Heirs of Fixed Destiny

Book Ninc
of
The Return of the Tribes

By A. A. Taylor

First Edition

The Rum Lot Publishing
Lowestoft, Suffolk, UK
2025

ISBN 978-1-918079-25-8
Paperback Edition

Books of this series are available for download on

Amazon Kindle
or
The Rum Lot Publishing
www.rumlot.com

Fairies black, gray, green, and white,
You moonshine revelers and shades of night,
You orphan heirs of fixèd destiny,
Attend your office and your quality.

The Merry Wives of Windsor
Act 5, Scene 5

By William Shakespeare

Book Nine

1697, The Fortuneteller

The winter of 1697-98 was extraordinarily cold in the German Margraviate of Ansbach, and on a particularly miserable day the five-wagon Romani clan was camped well outside the city walls. They were desperate to continue their journey to a warmer climate but were late in setting off. Mari had given birth and was in a bad way, and they were forced to settle in for a couple of weeks. By the time they started their winter migration south the winter goddess Marzanna had other ideas.

The Fortuneteller wouldn't leave the young couple and their baby behind, so everyone waited, and while there was a bit of grumbling, she was the leader, she was the elder, and she was the witch. There was no argument, at least not to her face. In their hearts, even as they grumbled, the other three families knew she'd do the same for them.

It was Yule, the shortest day of the year, and that morning four men rode to the little encampment – three soldiers and a very well-dressed man with a sour and superior face, the castle's Stat-Halter. He was in charge of running the castle and was the top manager for Margrave William Frederick.

The Fortuneteller walked out to meet him, and she knew right away that he didn't want to talk to a woman, but that was his problem, not hers, and she stood her ground.

"I want," he snapped, without any greeting or introduction, "your fortune teller. I was told one lived here with you people. A lady in the castle wants to talk with one."

He spat the words out like they were poison, and to him, they probably were.

"What does she want? And will she pay?"

His face turned a lovely shade of burgundy at her tone, which said she was talking to an equal, but his voice was even. His horse could feel his master's upset and snorted. "She wants to ask one question. She will pay three gold coins."

Three gold coins were a lot. But not enough to die for, and if The Fortuneteller went to the castle, how would she know she'd make it back out? By definition, anyone who went to "answer a question" could be denounced as a witch, and the Germans were still burning and hanging them. Burning a witch or two was good fun. It broke up the dark days of winter.

"It's a generous offer, but no thank you. We'll be leaving in the morning, and we have a lot to do."

"You'll take the offer. I guarantee your safety if that's your concern. You'll leave tomorrow. But I don't guarantee your safety," and he looked at the small clan standing silently behind her, "or the safety of your family if you refuse."

The Fortuneteller sighed. An offer she couldn't refuse. They only had three men and two stripling boys. And her. They couldn't fight off the castle soldiers if the Stat-Halter decided to clear out some Romani witches. No one would question his decision.

"Well, put that way, I see I have no choice. I will accept your offer of three gold coins. Are you a man of God, Stat-Halter?"

"Of course, I am!" He spat out the words like they were nails.

"Then promise as a man of God your guarantee of safe passage for me and my family. These men are witnesses."

"Of course, I promise."

So she shrugged and took the long walk through the falling snow to the castle. It was already getting dark.

In the castle, the Stat-Halter took The Fortunteller to a small private chapel of all places. Did they expect her to make a blood sacrifice on the altar to Satan or something? Or did they think her evil magic wouldn't survive there? Either way, they would be disappointed.

Like all the old churches, there were no pews, just a couple of chairs for the highest nobility, and even then, they were only used if the aristocrat was old or ill.

The Fortuneteller sat on a small bench in the very back, probably the leper's bench if they ever allowed such unclean people in the same room with the high and mighty. The chapel had a few cheap tallow tapers lit for light, but that was all. There was no heat, of course, and the Fortuneteller shivered, but her internal fire kept her from freezing.

After an hour, a side door opened, and a matronly, well-fed woman walked in with a pretty girl of about fifteen or so.

They looked around, and then the woman gasped and grabbed the girl by the arm; they both saw the Fortuneteller glowing in the back of the chapel, her green fire flashing over her body and her eyes two bright emerald beacons. They thought she was a demon from hell. If only! She was freezing her ass off, and for a few minutes, the fires of hell would have been a welcome change.

"What's your question?" The Fortuneteller was too cold for niceties, and she didn't expect any invites for tea and a rubber of whist from these two.

"We have two questions." Oh, good – they were already breaking the agreement.

"The first is to read this girl's future, and the second is to –" and her voice broke, "tell me what happened to the soul of my dead son. Is he in heaven? Limbo? A ghost?"

The Fortuneteller sighed. One of those mother-of-dead-children clients. Okay, best get this over with. She glared at the girl and read her fortune. The girl shivered, but not from the cold.

"You're going to marry a very highborn man. It'll be a happy marriage, and you'll have enough children. But only if you are well-educated and stop being a little snot. If you're lazy and continue being spoiled, then I don't know. A different path."

Then she looked at the woman. "I can't read the fortunes of the dead, but I do know your son is not a ghost. He is not wandering this world, so that means he is in the next, where he should be. Past that, I don't know. No one but the gods knows what happens on the other side of the Gates."

She nodded and walked up to the Fortuneteller, took a gold coin out of her purse and threw it on the ground, where it rolled and clattered. Then she stepped back and glared, her eyes challenging the witch to say anything. The Fortuneteller glowered back, angry. A cheat. A snotty cheat at that.

"The Stat-Halter told me three gold coins for one question, and I have answered two. Three coins is what we agreed."

The woman was haughty; she wasn't going to be told anything by a Gypsy witch. "I didn't agree to that, and you didn't tell me where my son was."

The purse flew out of the woman's hands, smacked into the Fortuneteller's, and the woman gasped and fell to her knees.

"Now you listen to me, you cheat. I told you what I know. Now I also know you can set your soldiers on me and my people, but listen and mark my words. You Germans have burnt many witches, some of them in front of this castle, but not one, *not a single one* was a real witch." The Fortuneteller's voice trembled with rage, and her whole body flamed.
"*But I am!* If you hurt one hair of my people, if you bother me in any way, I'll come back for you and this girl. You won't like that. You will spend eternity in a place where your son will not go. You won't like that either."

Her voice thundered. "*DO YOU UNDERSTAND!*"

The woman sobbed. Yes, she understood. The terrified girl cried and cowered, clinging to the woman.

The Fortuneteller snuffed the candles out with her magic and sped from the chapel and hysterical women, trotting as fast as she could through the pitch-black town, the heavy snow coming down in fat, wet flakes.

She was furious, and it was probably that fury that created the next incident of the night.

She ran into two watchmen, soldiers guarding the town, and when they saw her running down the cobbled streets, her body and eyes were glowing from her rage and growing fear for her clan.

One chased her, and he cornered her in a blind niche between two buildings. When she turned back to look at him, he cried, "WITCH!" And he pulled out a cross and held it up, and in the other hand, he held his sword. With a great swing, he lunged at her. She dodged. He missed.

The soldier regained his balance and leaned back to swing again. His eyes froze, he gasped, blood gushed from his mouth, then he collapsed to the ground like a sack of bricks.

The Fortuneteller killed him with her magic, the first time she had ever done such a thing. She'd ripped open the veins in his neck.

His companion knelt by the dying soldier, blood spraying over the white snow as his last heartbeat pumped, and, horrified, he looked up at the Fortuneteller. She saw a man in complete terror.

"Go," she whispered. "Go and live."

He leapt up and ran back the way he came, and she ran in the opposite direction, out through the town's gates and down to the forest where she pounded on the doors of the caravans and told them to hitch up; they had to leave *now*!

They drove hard all night, a nightmare journey through a strengthening blizzard, but by morning no one could follow their trail, and Ansbach was in the past. She never went back there.

There were fifteen gold coins in the pouch, and she shared them equally with each family. The coins bought some good, warm clothing and some fine new draft horses. Well worth it, in the end.

The Fortuneteller

The Fortuneteller could not tell her own fortune. Never could. That was the ultimate irony, and it was not lost on her.

She could see the futures of normal people, and, oh, gods, they were easy to read. Some futures were as plain as the nose on your face, and any fool could read them. A drug addict? Easy to figure out the path that life was going to take. A nun? Equally easy, although she had seen surprises. An old man in his eighties with yellow eyes and a lump in his belly? Anyone could see the fate of that person.

A newborn baby? Now that little human was a bundle of infinite possibilities. Not a blank slate; no one was. There were always some obvious influences like rich parents or something like a birth defect, but the web of paths that a new soul could take was mind-boggling.

And that's all telling futures was – looking down paths, weighing up possibilities, editing the story to adjust for whatever knot or kink she could see spring up on the rope of time. If the Fortuneteller drew a map of anyone's life, it would look like a river delta. The water of time would spring out of one central birthing point, split off into a right or left branch, and each of those branches would split off. Soon there wouldn't be one river but hundreds, thousands of possible rivers fanning out and sometimes merging again on their path to the sea – the Void – where it was everyone's fate to sooner or later be recycled and reborn.

The Fortuneteller's job was to find the main channel out of all the possible channels and suss out the rocks and rapids that changed the course of the flow of time. Time could not be stopped; of course, it only moved forward, but each path you took on your journey could be altered, and that was the result of billions of decisions made by yourself and others. The Fortuneteller could, maybe, give a bit of information that could nudge you in one direction or another, and that would change everything. Time was immutable, but free will had immense power, too.

A few years earlier, she'd read the news out of England about the miracle of the reappearance of the elves and lords. It explained a lot, that blank spot she had seen lately when she read some futures. Some people, not many, had empty places in their futures. It was hard to explain, but the river delta would have smudges; possibilities were there but not there and couldn't be read. Then the lords came, and she tried, just for fun, to read their futures, and she couldn't. Total fog. The lords existed, but their timelines were coy, there but hidden. Just like hers.

Her theory was that the average people who came to her, who had blank spots that hinted at possible futures, were somehow intertwined with the lords or elves. It made sense even if it made her job a bit harder, but that was the fun, the challenge, and goodness knows she needed a bit of a challenge to keep her from being lazy. She had learned long ago that when she stopped telling fortunes, she didn't feel good, and she aged. The wrinkles and patchy hair weren't so bad because, hey, she was old. But the aches and pains of ageing weren't fun, and if telling a fortune or two kept her knees from yelling at her, that was worth the effort.

Today, if someone looked at her closely, they'd say she was in her late forties, but if she did hard magic every day – if she really exercised – she soon looked like she was in her early thirties. She had one of those young faces.

Early in her life, the struggle to survive meant constant, daily challenges, and she would never say her life was dull. Awful at times, but not dull. Now it was dull.

People still came to her for readings, and there was nothing much new to learn from them. She had been telling fortunes for so long that she had met everyone, absolutely everyone, who had an interesting, novel story, and now their stories were on endless reruns. There were so few new stories (her clientele was an unending line of chubby, middle-class matrons and giggly college coeds enjoying a girl's night out) that looking into their futures was repetitive and boring.

"Your new accountancy job will be cut short by forces out of your control. I'd save up a stash of cash if I were you. Your daughter is going to get pregnant next year, so that will take some money, too."

"You'll graduate and move to Iowa, where you'll marry a guy who's an electrical contractor and have three kids."

"Avoid anyone driving a green Ford Fiesta."

She wouldn't tell her customers if something horrible was going to happen that they couldn't avoid. You didn't keep repeat customers if they left scared and depressed, and what good would it do to tell someone their possibilities were going to end in six months in a head-on car crash? Would they avoid driving? No, after a few weeks of terror, they'd rationalise the Fortuneteller's prediction, say she was a batty old woman, and get back in a car. And they would die anyway. Free will was there, but if you don't use it, you stay trapped in the river currents of time. Most people didn't take her seriously, and she was fine with that.

Every now and then, the Fortuneteller would change the course of time, help an open-minded, deserving person use their free will, and something good would happen. She liked steering people into happy marriages.

"Take a second look at John in Accounts Receivable. He's a keeper!"

Or she'd tell the coeds to start sending their resumes to ad agencies in San Francisco; they'd find a job there, not in New York. That sort of thing. And occasionally they'd come back with wonder in their eyes and tell her that they were moving to San Francisco for their dream job and thank her. That was fun, and her green eyes would glitter with amusement, and they would leave, scared, and never return. When coloured contacts were invented, that was a godsend.

She couldn't read her own fortune, but she could sometimes infer her own fate from the fortunes of others who crossed her path because the river delta of time wasn't two-dimensional and flat; it was layered, and other people's futures (and free will) affected her own.

Many times in her life, she would look at a clan member, and suddenly that person's future would hit her so hard that she would gasp, lose all air, and the pain would pound her to her knees. The most recent time, one of the worst, was in 1942 when many of her small clan booked passage out of Romania on the MV Sturma. Most of the other passengers were Jewish, but the Nazi concentration camps were equally cruel to the Roma gypsies, and when Ephraim came to the camp waving tickets, gleeful to tears that he had saved his family, it was all she could do to stay conscious. In front of her eyes, he turned into a wraith, a ghost, an undead, and with growing horror, she watched him talk to the clan, telling the terrified families to pack up what they could carry; they were all going to Palestine.

He was furious when she stood up and told him and everyone else she wouldn't go and that the journey would end in death. "Staying here will end in death, too! The Germans are coming for us now!" But she refused to go, and there was a lot of screaming by him and the others who were desperate to flee and save their children. They cried that she was a crazy, old witch who didn't know what she was talking about, and all but one family left with him. She had no credible alternative to offer, and all her glowing eyes and portents of doom did was scare them away. To the men and women, their only choice was between the safety of Palestine or the death camps of the Germans, and by the next morning, almost everyone was gone.

On the twelfth of December in 1941, the MV Sturma, a small ship only about 150 ft long and 19 ft wide, left Constanta with seven hundred and ninety-one souls on board. Dreadfully overloaded for the four-day cruise, the hell-ship had no food or sanitation. Because of engine trouble, it took them until February 21st just to leave the Black Sea, and that was only because the Turkish navy towed them. On the south side of the Bosphorus Strait, on February 24th, the Turks dropped the tow line and returned home. Almost immediately, the doomed ship was torpedoed by the Germans, and everyone died.

Every last one.

There was no point to the murder other than that the Germans didn't want the suffering Jews and Roma civilians to live. Her clan had avoided the torture of the death camps to die by the Nazis on an equally torturous death boat.

The Fortuneteller led the last ten of her clan to safety. Every few weeks, she would lead them somewhere new, just ahead of the Nazis and the equally bad Russians, evading sure death from either bullet or systemic genocide.

When the river of possibilities showed doom, they would pack up and take their three tiny caravans down the rutted back roads, fighting off other desperate refugees and grim farmers who would shoot at trespassers, trying to keep their own families alive. She would sit on the first caravan, urging the tired, rough horse to her next goal and watching the people driving or walking by. As they passed the three slow caravans, she would read their futures. If their future showed them turning down a road to the left and dying, she would go right. If the constant ant trail of refugees and lost souls were going to run into a battle or a Nazi patrol, she knew it, and they would avoid following those people.

Slowly – it took months – the ten remaining, traumatised, starving members of her clan ended up in Portugal, where they eked out a bare survival until the end of the war. Two years after the war ended, they had scraped up enough money to book passage for all of them (Fifteen now; children had been born!) to the US.

It was hard getting everyone into the US. The war was over, and the Romani were still despised, but they managed. There were Romani in the US, and amongst them, they found sponsors to help with the bureaucracy because how could they not help their own people?

Nowadays, passports have photographs, and the Fortuneteller had a devil of a time getting an acceptable photograph; everyone also needed birth certificates. Every last one of them was born in the back of a movable house, and half the time, the parents couldn't even remember which country they had stopped in when their children were born.

It wasn't the money that kept them in Portugal; it was the paperwork. But in the end, they bribed, wrangled, and begged passage, and she even brought over her old caravan, although she had to sell her horse. From the Fortuneteller's point of view, the

Americans had plenty of horses, but a three-hundred-year-old Roma caravan to live in? No. And she was right.

America was good to them. While there was still an occasional ugly incident (Gypsies, as they were called, weren't loved anywhere), it was a world away from the horrors of Europe. Eventually, her clan blended in with the other Romani who had been in America for centuries and the new ones who had fled the Porajmos and dribbled over to the US.

Most of her clan ended up settling in Texas, where they bought a couple of good ranches outside of Houston and only travelled to work the fairs, festivals, and their own reunions. They did well and had lots of children, most of whom the Fortuneteller didn't know. To them, she was a myth they met once a year for a few minutes, and after a decade or two, the legends faded and were forgotten by the next generation, and that was fine with the Fortuneteller. She didn't want a seventy-year-old to remember meeting her when he was a child and wondering why the Fortuneteller was still around and why she still looked thirty-five.

After ten years of roaming around the US telling fortunes at fairs, the Fortuneteller moved to Chicago with the very last of anyone she could call her kin. Her however-many-great-grandniece married a gadjo (non-Romani) guy from there, and it seemed to be as good a place as any to put down roots. She bought a nice little house on a busy street with a garage to store her caravan, hung out a sign on the front porch that said *Fortuneteller*, and talked to whoever walked in the front door – for a price. Reading fortunes kept her young, paid for the occasional trip to the reunions, and supported her few needs. After years of fleeing pogroms, slavery, witch burnings, and garden-variety meanness and abuse, it was good to have time and space to breathe, sleep, and dream in safety.

But time moves forward, and in the great ebb and flow of life, where joy dims to sadness and back to joy, everything else swings to and fro as well, and now safety and calm were swinging back to terror. The Fortuneteller could feel the change coming like a cold Norther blowing off Lake Erie.

Chicago was her home for over seventy years, and that was by far the longest she had ever stayed in one place. Her niece was long gone, along with her niece's grandchildren, and she was totally alone. Deliberately alone. She hadn't been to a reunion for almost twenty years.

In her long life, the Fortuneteller had found it necessary to occasionally cut all ties from old families and find new ones. When her age didn't match her looks, and people started questioning, it was just easier to fade away. Not abruptly, but she didn't have any husband or children, and if people lost track of an old maiden auntie – well, that just happened, didn't it? In all of her years on this Earth, not a single person ever tried to track her down after she went missing for a few years. As much as her clans were fond of her, they had their own lives and closer kin to worry about. And the Fortuneteller was a bit uncanny, even for the Roma.

She had been thinking about moving on for a few years because she knew she was nesting for far too long; then the lords and elves came back. When Lord Cadence made the news, the Fortuneteller had a shock of recognition so profound that it knocked her off her feet, and it took a week for her to get settled again. Here was a woman who looked like her, ears and all! And she wasn't a one-off weirdo, either. There was a man. And in the coming year, there was news of others.

There was a nation of them.

The Fortuneteller, who for hundreds of years was considered by her own people to be a witch, a demon, a fairy, a djinn, or an imp, wasn't alone in the world. She had a tribe.

She couldn't begin to say how that made her feel, and every emotion she felt had its opposite. Happy? Yes, but terrified, too. She was no longer unique, and she was no longer alone. There were male lords out there, and that brought its own terrors and anticipations.

Those lords had powers totally different from hers, so was she going to be a weak one who was dominated, or would she have value and equality in a new clan? Her people were once slaves, and she wouldn't be anyone's slave. Not again, not ever.

And the little people, the elves. Oh. My. Stars. There was something in just knowing that they existed that made her long to see one, to touch them, like a drug addict looking at a rock of crack. If she went to live with the elves, would she ever be able to leave them? The pull was undeniable, and she was wise enough and old enough to know that the longing she felt wasn't a passing fancy, but something much, much deeper.

She dithered. If this were a normal client, she would read their fortune, trace the possibilities, and she'd know immediately whether the person on the other side of the table was walking into danger or a blessed community. But she couldn't read her own fortune, and she had spent her entire life avoiding traps. She had been stolen once and kept as a slave, and once was enough. After that, slavery never trapped her again, but it had happened to others. Roma were slaves in some parts of Eastern Europe until the 1860s.

But now she was in agonies of indecision, fear, elation, insecurity, hope – it was all there.

Too many options. Too many possible outcomes. Too much unknown. Too much danger to risk her hard-won, comfortable, and safe life.

On the other hand, she was bored and lonely, and the pull of the elves and a community was very, very strong. She spent hours on the internet flipping through elf sites and reading the Elf Nation info pages.

But it wasn't just the elves that gave her itchy feet. Around her life was suddenly getting dangerous, just like the 1930s in Europe. When the "Act for Humanity" bill was introduced, she started seriously making preparations to move. In 1930, she should have moved to the US then, when the shit in Eastern Europe started, but she didn't. The Fortuneteller would not make that mistake again.

Where she should go, she didn't know, but now the US was not so safe anymore. All those decades ago, the Weimar Republic's instability and Fascist ideas that had permeated Europe and made it not so safe, and the Fortuneteller could see the obvious parallels. Ideas and talk could always turn into action, and real peril came to a head with the Nazis in '33. She wasn't going to wait for the Nazis to show up in Chicago and stand on her doorstep, pounding on her door.

But she was too slow, and in front of her eyes her paths narrowed and possibilities were quickly cut off. A lord was shot while trying to get into Canada without a passport. The Fortuneteller's ancient passport couldn't be renewed because the minute it was sent in, the government would know she was a lord because of the fuzzy photo. Her old documents had a fake birthdate on them, 1901, that worked at the time, but now she would be seen as being well over a hundred and thirty years old. Gods help her if anyone found out she really was born in 1590.

The only place she could slip over the border without a passport was either Canada or Mexico, and as sure as shit she couldn't go through a legitimate border post. The gunned-down lord proved that. Just like when she left Portugal in 1947, she needed the paperwork to permit passage, and now documents were all computerised. She had no idea how to get a fake passport. She knew criminals managed, but if they were caught, they were denied passage or, at worst, fined, detained, and deported. She would be killed.

Then that bastard Meechum shut down the internet. The Fortunteller was pretty techy for an old bitch, and she kept up with what was going on in the world and read the news. Before the US government filtered them out, she read the elf gossip sites. So after the internet went down and censorship rose up, she knew that any emails or communications she sent to the EN would be intercepted. Having lived through the Nazis, she wasn't going to allow herself to be noticed by snitches and local government agents. She didn't want her name put on a list. She didn't want anyone with a badge or a job sitting in a cubicle to notice her.

Being noticed for who she was was death. They, whoever "they" were, were always trying to kill her. That never changed.

The noose was tightening, and she had to make a decision: go north or south, and then Mexico decided for her. They weren't anti-lord or elf, not like the US was fast becoming, but somebody in Mexico City decided that they should find and register all the lords in order to protect them from kidnappers, crazies, and the US government. In other words, a Mexican bureaucrat decided they needed to make a list.

So north to Canada.

The Fortuneteller saw the announcement on the news about Mexico, and a half hour later, she was in her garage packing. She didn't have a car and didn't even know how to drive, but she had hundreds of years of experience with horse-and-wagon rigs, and it wasn't hard to go back to that mode of transportation.

Carefully stored in the ramshackle garage was her old caravan, the one she'd brought with her from Portugal, a lovely piece of hand-crafted traditional art that she had owned for over three hundred years. Oh, there probably wasn't a single piece of original old wood on it, with a rebuilt stave here and a replaced wheel there over that vast time, but as it stood now, it was perfect and perfectly able to be used. She hadn't allowed a spot of rust or a woodworm to live on it since it was pushed into the garage, and every time something looked tired and old, it was restored or replaced. She loved her caravan; it was gorgeous. But it wasn't its beauty that made her obsessively keep it in perfect condition; it was what it meant. It was her last-ditch escape route, her key to a safe life. Her key to life, period.

When you flee your first witch hunter at the age of ten, you never let down your guard. The Fortuneteller will never forget being trapped in the stinking crush of a howling mob and watching a screaming witch tortured and burnt to death. The Germans stopped executing witches in 1775, and Poland stopped in 1790. For the first two hundred years of her life, she'd avoided being burned as a witch, and the lessons learned during those years never left her.

She never had a car, so no license that had her name and age in a database. She never paid into Social Security or paid taxes. She never had a mortgage or a bank account, and while her deed had her name on it, it didn't have her age. But it was getting old, and one day a computer would look at the unchanging name attached to that address and wonder why the same person had owned the same house for an un-human number of years. She paid for absolutely everything in cash and only took cash, much to the dismay of her current clients. Back in the fifties, she'd signed up for electricity under a fake name, and ever since then, every new utility account that needed verification and an ID was built on the back of that. It was a web of deceit that worked as long as she never had a late payment, and she never did.

The Fortuneteller was as far off the grid as it was possible to be and still live in the middle of Chicago.

She'd stay totally off the grid since new cars were all tracked with sat-navs and such, but her caravan wasn't. She wouldn't even need to buy gas. The caravan was an eye-catcher, and travelling with it and draught horses would bring all sorts of attention to her, but in a way that would be the ultimate disguise. No one would expect a lord to escape to Canada in about as unconventional and flashy a get-up as a red and gold, hand-carved, Romani caravan. Hiding in plain sight was how she'd managed her life in Chicago and something she had done many times in her life; she was used to it. But it meant constantly reading the public for information, which was tiring but in the end made her stronger and younger. It also meant being clever and on her toes all the time. Witches hid in the shadows, so a person standing in the limelight couldn't possibly be a witch, now could they?

The next day, she put her house up for sale for a ridiculous, cash-only price, and that afternoon was spent on the internet looking for draught horses. Within three days, she had a cash sale (her lawyer bought it for his son, a bit shady, but oh, well…), the money was transferred, her wagon was packed, and a power of attorney was written up so her lawyer could close on the house for her. The house was worth almost half a million, but she sold it for half of that "because she had a disease, no heirs, and wanted to splash out on the vacation of a lifetime." The fatal disease was an allergy to dying because she was a demon-witch, but the lawyer's son didn't need that detail.

The horses cost ten grand each, and she had six delivered to her on spec with a guaranteed purchase of four, cash. With some half-hearted haggling, she got the delivery thrown in for free. She wasn't looking for show animals but steady ones with good temperaments and already broken in to pull a wagon.

She was really pleased with the horses when they showed up and kept five because she just couldn't make up her mind. The caravan only needed two to pull it; the others were for spares, bad hills, and to carry packs of extra provisions. When they weren't pulling the caravan, they would be tied to the back and just follow along.

Before anyone noticed that the Fortuneteller was keeping five draught horses in her tiny backyard in urban Chicago, she was gone.

The Fortuneteller

If he studied maps of pre-industrial villages, a clever reader could see a pattern. Villages tend to be about twenty miles apart, and that's because twenty miles is the distance a draught team can haul a loaded wagon in a day. Twenty miles from where the Fortuneteller lived barely got her out of Chicago. It certainly didn't get her out of the suburbs.

She had speculated about how to manage a caravan journey out of Chicago for years, but more as a thought exercise for entertainment than as a real, life-dependent escape. She'd mused about taking the caravan south, maybe to a reunion or festival, but now that the journey was serious, she was going north to Canada. Luckily, Chicago was reasonably close to Canada. What if she had settled in Miami!

Idle speculation now turned into practical planning, and the most immediate decision was to take the smallest, least-travelled back roads she could find and go from commercial campground to campground until the towns thinned out and she could find quiet parks and rest stops to overnight in.

She needed a place for the horses to rest, some rough grass for grazing, and water for them. And she needed a campground that would be so charmed with her fantastic caravan and the gorgeous draught horses that they would forgive a few ruts from the wheels and some torn-up lawn from grazing horses. From her experience with attending the Romani reunions and festivals, that was not an unrealistic hope.

There was even a story ready to use, because every entertainer needs a script, and the Fortuneteller knew that she needed to answer any question with confidence and without overthinking it. She tells everyone she was a Romani reenactor, following a trail her ancestor took, and living authentically off the grid. She'd let people take photos of the caravan and horses but not of herself "because it was bad luck." In reality, the Roma didn't give a crap, but it certainly would be bad luck for the Fortuneteller to be caught on camera as a fuzzy, unphotographable lord, so she hoped that one would work.

It was six hundred and thirty miles, or about six weeks, to the Canadian border in Minnesota, and four hundred and seventy miles, or about a month, to Sault Ste Marie if she went through Michigan. It was September, and she was heading north; she couldn't afford any delays, or she'd be stuck on the wrong side of the border during winter, and the horses would suffer.

The exact route would be determined in a few days after seeing how things went and what the possibilities looked like.

Leona

Leona was absolutely floored when the Gypsy drove her magnificent wagon into the Sleepy Pines RV Park and Campground. It was like watching something out of a movie; two huge Belgian draught horses pulled the most fantastic Gypsy caravan, followed by a train of three more draught horses loaded with packs. The last horse had a big fluorescent pink triangle tied to its butt that said "SLOW! HORSES!" on it.

The caravan pulled up to the Reception Office, and out hopped a woman dressed in heavily embroidered skirts, red leather boots, and a white embroidered blouse. On her head, she wore a turban. Leona had never seen so much jewellery on a human being in her life. Necklaces, bangles, earrings, coins sewn everywhere. She jingled as she walked, so there must have been a few bells hidden in the glittering mess.

Leona pegged her at about forty, maybe younger, maybe older. It was hard to tell. She was unconventionally attractive, though, with a heart-shaped face decorated with a quick, wide smile, huge, liquid brown eyes, and a dimple in her chin.

"Hi!" The Gypsy smiled and waved as she walked up to the door, her ringed fingers glittering in the sun. "I don't have a reservation because I don't have a phone, but do you have a rough camping area I can rent for the night? I don't need a bunk or anything, just a place on grass to park." There was an accent, faint and indescribable, but Leona could tell that English was not her first language.

The manager didn't know what to say at first because they'd never had a team of horses just walk up like this, but after thinking about it, she assigned a quiet corner in the long grass, which the Gypsy lady said was perfect, and she asked if the horses could graze on the grass there. Leona didn't see why not, and that made everyone happy.

By the time the wooden wagon was in place, the entire park had wandered by to take a look. It was shoulder season, so the kids were back in school, and the campers were mostly snowbirds heading south, but even the oldies loved looking at the wagon, gingerly petting the horses, and talking to the Gypsy reenactor. It was quite an attraction. Everything was absolutely authentic, and the woman was happy to talk about the caravan and the history of the Roma people. She knew so much it was almost as if she had lived it.

All she asked was that no photos be taken of herself, but the caravan and the horses were fine. Bad luck, she said, and smiled and winked. "I'll put a Gypsy curse on you, so no cheating!" And everyone laughed and did as she said.

She staked the horses out so they could graze on the long grass, and she asked one of the older guests to watch her caravan while she filled up buckets of water for them. This immediately garnered volunteers, and she didn't have to go get the water herself. Even the buckets were charming and authentic! Two guests asked to buy one, and the Gypsy grinned and said no, she didn't have time to replace them if she sold them. But maybe one day –

It took over an hour, but eventually all the horses were watered and had feed bags buckled on, and the woman brushed them down with quick, practised strokes.

Soon it was dark, and the campers drifted back to their own campsites. Leona stopped by to wish the woman a good night and ask how long she was going to stay. They talked about the next campsite, and Leona told her which would be the best one and offered to call in a reservation, and her help was gratefully accepted. All the nearby campsites knew each other, she said, because if one was full up they'd refer the guests to the nearest one with a space. Twenty miles was nothing in a car, but it was a full day of work for the horses, and if she just asked Leona was sure the Gypsy would always be able to find a spot twenty miles down the road.

The last Leona saw of the Gypsy, she was bending over a tiny fire and stirring something in a pot. When Leona drove in the next morning, the campsite was bare, and all that she could see were the ruts where the wagon had sat and circles of mown grass where the horses had grazed.

The Elf Nation

The Elf Nation AI combed the internet constantly looking for pictures that could be evidence of a lord. The elves had developed a special program that could look at a blurry photo and sharpen it, even if the fuzziness was because of the magic energy aura that surrounded an elf or lord. When the Fortuneteller stopped at the campsite, the few campers who wandered over to her caravan to wonder and look were respectful, just as she'd asked. They didn't take any direct photos of her, but one person did take a picture of the lovely horses while the Gypsy was on the other side, brushing them down.

The woman who took the picture was careful not to offend, and the huge horse hid almost all of the Fortuneteller's body.

Almost.

The bottom of the skirt and the red boots could be seen through the horse's legs, and that's all the AI needed. When the photo was loaded up on the camper's Instagram page and labelled "Gypsy Caravan and Draft Horses" with a geolocation, the automatic filters shunted the photo into a folder for closer examination by an elf, curled up with her tablet and working from home in her sitting room in Scotland. That wasn't just camera blur; that was magic blur. The elf was intrigued – who wore magic boots?

The computer was told to search for all photos of the Gypsy caravan, and thirty-four were spit out. Two more had tiny, blurry sections to them. A bit of skirt, half a hand.

But a third hit paydirt. It was of the caravan on the road, taken by a passenger in a passing car. The wagoneer sat hidden in the door of the caravan, the loose reins looped around a knob. A human looking at the photo would just think the driver was lost in the shadows. An elf saw the blur of magic, and when the filters took away the blur, there she was. A lord.

She was wearing red boots.

Two hours after the first photo was uploaded to Instagram, an emergency meeting was convened, and in Ottawa, Gen Jameson was alerted that a lord was seen moving north in Illinois and would probably be crossing the border into Wisconsin the next day. Luckily, he still had a small team of human operatives in Lethbridge, and two were assigned to the case.

Four hours after the photo first hit Instagram, a Ranger walked into a safe house in Sault Ste Marie. It was one in the morning, but hey, that's what overtime was for. A half hour later, she was gone.

Darnya

Darnya was ported to Sault Ste Marie, where she was provided with an old car, camping supplies, and a clean Canadian passport. Like a lot of footloose Canadians, she was heading to Florida for the winter months to work in the tourist trade. Probably Boca. She liked the town, but if she couldn't find a job waitressing there, then she'd try Port St Lucie.

She camped as she drove south because it was fun and because it was a lot cheaper than getting a motel.

The Gypsy-lord was moving north as fast as two huge Belgians could haul a wooden mobile home, which averaged about two miles an hour when you figured in rest stops and water breaks, barely over the pace of a leisurely stroll. Darnya anticipated intercepting her sometime that morning, and she didn't expect any issues with that.

The Fortuneteller

Up with the chickens at six, the Fortuneteller was on the road, following the back roads on her paper map and debating to herself whether or not she should risk activating her phone. The police shows on TV always had them tracking down suspects with their cellular activity, and she just didn't know if pinging a satellite to find out if there were any traffic difficulties or construction zones ahead was worth the risk.

As it was, the roads she chose were clear, and traffic was blessedly light. While most of the time, she could hug the hard shoulder, occasionally, she had to tell the horses to move into traffic.

They were good horses, steady and not spooked by the cars, most of which were courteous and passed her with agonising care, but not all were so sensible and kind. Some were assholes. One driver with a bunch of high school boys on the way to football practise chose to lean on his horn just as he drove by the lead horse, but all he got in return was a disdainful equine stare back. The horse's name was Old Bob, and he told the Fortuneteller later that drivers like that should be driven from the herd, and she couldn't disagree. A few years isolated in a bachelor herd would do that one some good.

When the morning work traffic picked up a bit before eight, she pulled off onto a Walmart parking lot for an hour to wait for it to thin out and to give the horses a chance to rest a bit. The guys in the Walmart garden section hauled out a long hose, and she was able to water the horses and answer a few questions – and have pictures taken, of course. They also took down a grocery list, and she gave them the money (cash) to buy her some food, which was great. When she left, she had a good pile of hot food from the deli to snack on while the horses made their slow way north.

Darnya

During her drive south, Darnya had continual updates pinged to her from the intel elves. The Gypsy lord had three geo-located photos taken by cars passing her uploaded to the internet. Then the lord stopped at a Walmart, and that provided another flurry of pics. They were following her in real time, just as good as any of Maksym's trackers would have.

By ten am, Darnya intercepted her wagon, and the elves told her where she would be stopping for the night. The campground and RV park had entered a reservation for her into their computer, sent by a woman named Leona at the last park. Darnya now had a reservation at the same park, too.

Darnya drove past the caravan twice, taking photos with her dash cam, but after that, she just pulled off into a busy parking lot (when she could find one) and waited for the lord to meander by. She would have loved to shadow her, but it was just impossible to drive that slowly behind the horses and not be obvious. The lord would know she was being followed almost immediately, and Darnya didn't know what that would mean to the woman. The last thing she wanted to do was harass the lord and end up with a lord-grade meltdown like what had happened with Lord Ratna.

In the meantime, the elves in the Lord Extraction Group were trying to figure out where this one had come from. Was she born in the US, like Lord Sarah and the twins? Was she a 3,500-year-old Old Fart from Before Times?

Ethnic Romani gave birth at home, and in the past, a birth certificate wasn't considered important. They searched through birth records, newspaper clippings, social security records, and even old high school yearbooks. Nothing.

Then a filter through the passport records of the Romani who entered the US from Europe hit a likely name. Aethelind o Devinàtoro, born 1901, unknown city, Poland. Parents unknown. No birth certificate; entry was approved by a notorious under-consulate in Portugal who had sticky fingers. But what was most interesting was the photo in the passport records. It was blurry, and someone had obviously hand-drawn in the eyes. It would have barely passed inspection in 1947, and certainly would have been rejected today. Which is why it had to be approved by the right person – for a fee. The woman in the photo wore a cloche hat, which was old-fashioned for the day, and it conveniently hid her ears. The elves put the probability of this person being their unknown lord at 98%.

Aethelind o Devinàtoro. Aethelind the Fortuneteller.

The information was passed on to the extraction team.

So the day ended up with Darnya moving from parking lot to parking lot, waiting for the lord to pass by, and then dash out and leapfrog to the next waiting place and hope that she wasn't noticed.

Finally, when the shadows were getting long and it was obvious where the caravan was heading, Darnya sped ahead to the campground to sign in and set up her tent before the lord very, very slowly oozed in. She was glad Maksym wasn't with her today; he would have been going crazy. As it was, Darnya had been awake for almost twenty hours now, and she still had hours to go; working alone without anyone to spell you was hard. She could use a nap.

The Fortuneteller and Darnya

This campground was a lot like yesterday's, and the manager/owner, a Sikh named Ralph, was very accommodating. He knew the Fortuneteller was coming because Leona had called in a reservation, and he asked if she would like him to do the same since she didn't have a phone.

He really didn't understand the phone thing, and all the Fortuneteller could say, without lying or telling the puzzled manager she really did have a phone but she'd turned it off, was to say that it was her goal to be as authentic as possible. Misleading by omission, maybe, but not an outright lie she told herself.

Together they looked at her road map, and he told her where the campgrounds were, the pros and cons of each, and she pointed to one. Ralph said he'd take care of it, and that was that.

At least, the Fortuneteller thought, she was over the Wisconsin state line now. Progress was being made. Tomorrow she'd have to make a decision. Head west and north and go to Canada through Minnesota, or keep going due north and then east into Michigan. The Michigan route was a lot shorter, but going from Michigan to Canada was where that lord was shot and almost died. On the shorter eastern route, the options to sneak into Canada and avoid border patrols and outposts were much more limited.

She'd have to cross water, and the only bridge was in Sault Ste Marie, and that would be heavily guarded.

On the other hand, the longer western route, angling up through Minnesota, gave her access to thousands of miles of continuous prairie. Somewhere in that vast border would be a hole, and any border crossing would be on dry land.

She made camp, staked out the horses, and dealt with the onlookers. Tonight, there were a good number of retirees, but sprinkled in with them were two families with kids, and the kids were a handful. She had to tell the parents to watch the kids and not let them run around behind the horses in case they kicked.

A little girl, probably about six, didn't want her parents to hold her hand and screamed bloody murder.

"They won't kick me! If they kick me, I'll kick back!"

Her parents wouldn't tell her to mind her manners but tried to reason with her, and the child was not having any of it. In full purple-faced fury, she screamed at her mother, slapped at her father, and entertained the crowd with a total meltdown. The Fortuneteller had been around Romani kids for hundreds of years, and she had never seen such an out-of-control child in her life. Finally, she snapped.

"You must take this child away. If she kicks a horse, they'll blink. If a one-ton horse kicks her, she'll die. You've now been warned."

The girl's mom chose to be offended and told the Fortuneteller that it was a free country, and she couldn't order them off the campsite; the kids could play where they wanted. She let go of the girl's hand, and as fast as a ferret, the child ran up to the Fortuneteller and gave her a whacking big kick in the shin.

There was a collective intake of breath from the retirees, who had now stopped taking photos so they could watch the entire spectacle. All the Fortuneteller did was stand there open-mouthed. Then she closed it with a snap and took a deep breath. Ralph was running up the path; someone must have called him, but before he could get there, Darnya grabbed the girl and handed her to her mother.

"Lady, that's assault. You let her go, knowing full well your kid would attack this woman. If she doesn't press charges, I can, and I will. Take this little bundle of joy and get out of here while you can and still have custody of her."

A couple of the onlookers woke up and started yelling at the family to leave, and Ralph herded them all down the path. As they left, the Fortuneteller could hear the mom shrieking that their holiday was ruined, that no one should have horses in the camp, and it wasn't their fault – nothing had happened.

Darnya turned to the Fortuneteller. "Hey, I'm really sorry you had to put up with that. Loony parents – some people –" And she shrugged and stuck out her hand. "My name is Darnya. Is there anything I can help with? Little Miss Sunshine has messed up your routine. I'm happy to help you get caught up."

The Fortuneteller looked at the little woman, and the outstretched hand didn't waver. So she shook it and gave a weak smile. Darnya looked into her eyes and smiled back –

And the eyes were brown. Not female lord green. Brown.

"I was going to water the horses. If you could help me, that would be great."

Darnya was joined by three of the retirees, and they went to fill up buckets of water for the horses, and everybody was back in a good mood. Except for the Fortuneteller, she was suddenly nervous. What if the parents came back and caused trouble? What if they called the police? She hadn't done anything wrong, but Romani and the police were oil and water. The last thing she wanted was to be noticed in a bad way. To have her name put on a list.

"Maybe I should move on – " she murmured and walked over to the horses. They were tired, and if she left now, she'd be travelling in the dark, sharing the roads with cars, and risking an accident. Many times she had broken camp and crept out in the dark to escape some official or hostile mob, and it was never fun.

"Don't worry. I can move my tent over this way if you think the idiots might be back; we can share a watch. If you let me sleep first, you can wake me up around midnight, and you can grab some sleep before morning." Darnya set the bucket down and gave the horse (damn, they were big!) a good drink. "If anything comes up, I'll yell. You'll wake up."

The Fortuneteller considered this and patted the horse's neck. They needed a rest, and she could doze off in the wagon during the day. "That's very kind of you, Darnya."

"It's okay. I like camping, but single women in a tent need to watch out for each other, so I make camping buddies all the time. It's safer." Darnya shrugged and then looked at the Fortuneteller. "So what's your name anyway? I didn't catch it."

"Just call me the Fortuneteller." She smiled at Darnya. "*Hey, you* also works. With my people, we don't share our names easily. Don't take it personally. Maybe tomorrow."

Darnya was taken aback. No one had ever refused to share their name with her. But all she could do was shrug and move on. "Okay, that's fine. I'll go and move my tent here. Where would be a good place to pitch it?" And with that, they both went to work.

Late that night, when the Fortuneteller was in her caravan, presumably sleeping, and Darnya was on watch, she texted the entire conversation to the elves. A few minutes later, there was a reply, "The Romani people use two given names, a secret name and a public name. The public *gadžikano nav*, which is the non-Romani name, and the secret *romano nav*, which is the Romani name. The Romano Nav is the name used inside the Romani community, and sometimes not even their non-Romani friends and acquaintances know it. *The Fortuneteller* must be her *gadžikano nav.* Don't call her Aethelind until she gives you explicit permission."

Then the elf asked the obvious. "Do you think she's wearing coloured contacts?" And with that, Darnya realised she really needed someone to work with and spell her so she could sleep. Duh.

It was a good thing Maksym was on his way.

Darnya

Morning came, and when the Fortuneteller moved to break camp, Darnya already had her pitch ready. She hoped the Fortuneteller would buy it.

She brought over two cups of coffee and some doughnuts she had left over from the day before.

"Fortuneteller, I was thinking. It really makes me nervous to think of you being out on the road alone. Those idiots last night – well, yahoos like that get weird ideas. Do you mind if I tag along just for today?" Darnya looked up and furrowed her brow, putting on her most concerned just-being-a-friend face. "Now, before you say no, it's really no trouble. Ralph told me where your next camp is, and I'm only going twenty miles out of my way, and that's nothing in a car. Fifteen minutes."

The Fortuneteller sipped her coffee and thought about it. It wasn't like this Darnya was a bother; she really wasn't. And in the few conversations they had last night, she'd seemed sensible. She liked the woman. And she couldn't stop her anyway. But this overture was odd, and it didn't take any special talent to listen to her instincts that said there was more to this woman than it seemed on the surface. She looked straight at Darnya.

"Do you mean me any harm?"

Darnya knew exactly what was happening. The lord was asking her a direct question and testing to see if she was lying. You can't lie to a lord. The Fortuneteller knew what she was.

So the Ranger returned her steady gaze and didn't blink. "No. I'm legit and only want the best for you." And then the weirdest thing happened. She felt a wave pass through her, a flicker, a feeling of being – and she couldn't put her finger on it. It was odd, and if she wasn't talking to a lord, and if she didn't know she was being tested, she would have just thought the coffee wasn't agreeing with her. But it wasn't the coffee.

The Fortuneteller stood up, emptied the last bit of her coffee into the fire, brushed some leaves off her skirt, and then smiled at Darnya. The little woman's future was calm, at least for a few days, and it might be handy to have a person around to help. If nothing else, the Fortuneteller could use her like she had with the refugees when she fled the Nazi's, as a walking, talking alarm signal of dangers ahead and a guidepost to safer paths. If Darnya's future was okay, and the Fortuneteller followed her, then maybe her own future would be safer.

"If you want to travel with me for a day or two, that would be good. I'll welcome the company! But I warn you, the horses are slow. People are used to a much faster pace than I go. You'll get bored very soon."

Darnya grinned. This was easier than she thought it would be; she was sure the lord would brush her off, and then she'd have to figure out some other way to shadow her and keep her protected. Whatever test the lord put her through, she'd passed.

"Oh, I won't get bored! This is an adventure! I can tell my mother I was stolen by the Gypsies!"

The Fortuneteller didn't smile back and simply turned to the horses and started to hitch them up.

Darnya wasn't sure if she said something to make the Fortuneteller angry, but she had the niggling feeling she did.

Maksym and Darnya

Maksym met Darnya at the next campground, and he wasn't happy. There was, of all things, an orc family reunion going on, and the place was teeming with drunken, screaming, foul-mouthed idiots who were fast emptying the place of decent campers and driving the campground manager to distraction. He thought the man would eventually kick the goons out, but not soon enough for Maksym and certainly not soon enough to bring a lord in. If the Fortuneteller rode up, it would be like throwing a steak in a tiger pit.

They had no idea what sort of self-defence the lord was capable of and had no intention of finding out the hard way.

After frantically studying the local terrain on his phone, Maksym found another campsite only a mile away, a quiet, wooded corner behind a church and was phoning the minister when Darnya drove in. It took them an hour to go to the church, scope out the grounds, and arrange everything with the minister, who was happy to accommodate the re-enactor, especially after her advance team offered a hefty donation to the roof repair fund.

Then it took another half hour to figure out what to tell the lord. As Darnya pointed out, the lord knew she was a lord, and Darnya was sure the Fortuneteller could tell when people were lying. While the Ranger could catch her at lunch and tell her that the campground was packed with undesirables, as soon as the Fortuneteller started questioning Darnya about how she knew those people would be a particular danger to her and about the alternative site, there would be the lies and equivocations. No matter how well-meaning, they would immediately raise red flags.

Maksym sighed. They either let the woman walk right into a mess and hope no one was thrown in jail or discovered as an illegal magical creature and/or killed, or they simply come clean with the lord, tell her that the EN was trying to help her escape, and let the chips fall where they may. They sent an urgent report to Gen Jameson, and he agreed with their assessment, and they all agreed on what to do. Time to come clean.

The next thing to do was to get into their cars and drive down US 45 and look for the caravan. The Fortuneteller was gradually working her way west and trying to avoid the built-up areas bordering Lake Michigan, sticking to more rural roads, and she told Darnya she was going to try US 45. Darnya had put a tracker on the wagon, but for some reason, it wasn't working, so Maksym and Darnya drove down 45 for an hour, looking in every rest stop, Walmart, or fast food joint the lord could stop at to give the horses a break, and they couldn't find her. The elves were asked to keep a watch for posts of the caravan on social media. Nothing showed up. Not a peep.

Where yesterday it was wall-to-wall coverage of the Gypsy rig, today it was complete radio silence. They had lost her.

The Fortuneteller

When, for over four hundred years, you carry everything you own in a wagon – everything that keeps you alive – and there are people out to kill you, you get a bit obsessive with the condition of said wagon. The Fortuneteller was intimately familiar with her caravan and inspected the undercarriage every single day, sometimes two or three times a day if the terrain was rough. She knew how to fix, patch, rig, carve, and forge everything she needed to keep the thing rolling. Given time, a forge and good wood, she could even make a wheel if she had to.

So when Darnya stuck a tracker underneath the wagon, the Fortuneteller found it at the first rest stop after she left the campground. To her keen eye, it stuck out like a sore thumb. She didn't know if Darnya had put it there, but someone certainly had, and that meant she was being watched. If anything was going to spook this lord, a tracker certainly would.

As soon as she found the tracker, she drove to the back of the derelict strip mall where she had stopped to rest and smashed it with a hammer. Then, tidy person that she was, she tossed the shards in the garbage bin. After that, she went to the pack Young Bob was carrying and pulled out a tarp she had stowed just for this reason. The tarp was a white plastic case that covered the entire caravan, leaving only the wheels exposed. It had "Janet's Farm Fresh Organic Homemade Jam, Wholesale to Trade Only" written on both sides. Then she went inside the caravan and changed her clothes from Hollywood Gypsy to demure Mennonite Farm Girl and went on her way.

Since everyone (Darnya, the campground manager, and a few of the campers she had spoken to) knew she was going north up 45 to the next campground, she didn't. Instead, she took the smallest backroads she could find and went due west.

That night, she didn't stop at a campground but found a little rural church well off the road and camped in their parking lot. Romani knew what to look for, and finding a small, unguarded, unused building with a parking lot to pull into and stop for a few hours wasn't hard. She would be gone when dawn broke, before anyone drove in.

Maksym and Darnya

Maksym couldn't believe it. He and Darnya had once lost a lord walking with a superpack of white wolves in the Canadian wilderness, and now they'd lost a friggin' lord dressed as a Gypsy and driving a red and gold hand-carved caravan.

Pulled by five huge draught horses.

Moving at three miles an hour.

On a busy highway.

In one of the most congested urban corridors in the US.

If he wasn't careful, this could affect his Yule bonus.

At least no one could point to him and say he didn't know how to stick a tracker on; Darnya had done it this time, but it didn't make him feel better. He and Darnya were a team.

They spent all afternoon driving in ever-widening circles, futilely looking for the caravan. Then they spent all of the early evening cooling their heels in the campground just in case she showed up anyway. No success there, either, although it was entertaining to see the rent-a-cops deal with the extended orc family.

At nine, when it was too dark to trust the horses on the roads and they were sure the lord wasn't coming to the campground, they gave up and checked into a motel and got some sleep, determined to wake up at five and start searching again. Maybe during the night, the elves would come up with a lead.

They were both so upset they didn't even feel like screwing.

The Fortuneteller

Young Bob told the Fortuneteller he had sprung a shoe almost as soon as it happened. They were still making their way west on the backroads, and they hadn't gone six miles when Young Bob whinnied. She was able to pull off to the side and retrace their steps, and luckily, she found it. It wasn't far.

She asked him if he was hurt, and he said no, just off balance a bit, and she moved Louise up to pulling duty and rearranged the packs on the three trailing behind so that Young Bob didn't have a really heavy load. Then she started looking for a place to hide. Hairball complained about the extra weight, but by then, the Fortuneteller was learning the Belgian's personalities, and Hairball always complained about something.

Water was the big concern. She needed a quiet place to pull off where she wasn't too visible from the road, and it needed an unlocked water tap or a stream nearby. If it didn't have good grass on a lawn or verge, she could manage. Hairball, the complainer, was carrying plenty of grain, and while it was a bit rich to feed the horses nothing but grain, it would work for a day or two. She wouldn't get any complaints from the horses! She didn't carry water, though.

She kept her eyes peeled for a place that would work, but she was out in the middle of full-strength nowhere. The Fortuneteller drove the team up an arrow-straight country road, weaving her way between the towns of the Wisconsin Dells towards Madison and sticking to the most obscure backroads she could find, and she had found a good one.

In the last half hour, only one car had passed her. On both sides of the road were nothing but cornfields, occasionally interrupted by lanes that led to farmhouses and barns, set so far back off the road that they were just hints of humanity hidden in groves of mature trees, which were scattered clumps of dark green that peeked over the tall corn. She didn't see a soul, and the only sound was the wind and the rustling of cornstalks. If there were any people, they stayed hidden on their homesteads.

She wasn't going to go down a lane to a farmhouse and risk running into whoever lived there. She wasn't that desperate, so the Fortuneteller drove her team a slow, easy walk and admired the fields and the utter quiet of miles and miles of corn ripening in the sun, almost ready for harvesting.

Then she spotted it. A white equipment shed, a barn, just thirty yards off the road. There were no houses or anything around it, so it was obviously there so the farmer of the vast fields didn't have to go back to his house if he needed something while he was out in this part of his holdings. The huge metal shed was as neat as a pin, sitting in a large, mown lawn, and the grass was freshly cut. The Fortuneteller was sure it would have water there, too, being so close to the road and public water supplies. Water was probably why the farmer put it there in the first place, and not in the middle of the fields.

She turned in on the dirt driveway and pulled in behind the barn so she was hidden from the road. And there, in the middle of the steel wall, was a faucet with a neatly coiled industrial hose.

Perfect.

David

He was fixing a gate in the Townline fields when someone at the south barn set off the motion detector, and the alarm on his phone went off. It was the middle of the morning, so David didn't expect the usual equipment thieves breaking in, but no one should be there. He threw his tools in the back of the pick-up and sped off to see what was going on.

Probably kids. Or corn thieves. Sometimes, roving tourists in RVs stopped on the side of the road and swiped a dozen or so ears of the ripening corn, thinking it was sweet corn and not feed corn. If an RV had pulled into the barn's driveway and decided to have a rest stop, it wouldn't be the first time. He wouldn't mind, but some jerks left piles of garbage.

He certainly wasn't expecting what he found. As he pulled in the short driveway, a horse, a huge Belgian god-damn draught horse, walked around from the back of the barn and stared at him. That monster would certainly set off a motion detector.

As he opened his door and hopped out, another horse, even bigger than the first, came from behind the barn to stand by the first. Both stood and stared at the truck and the man. They didn't move.

Where the hell did they come from? He didn't know anyone nearby who kept heavy horses, not even the Plain people. The beasts ate too much to keep around just for a buggy, and a tractor on steel wheels wasn't considered too worldly and ploughed a sight better.

The horses whinnied, and he saw one look back. Then the other one took a step towards him, and David knew they were guarding something behind the barn. If he walked up to them and they took offence to his approaching, he would lose.

He started making soothing noises. Why, he didn't know, but when he was a kid and lived around horses, it was what you did when they got hostile. Horses were grazers, prey animals, and you had to tell them you weren't a threat. He walked up slowly, telling them he was okay, not to worry.

"They don't speak German. They speak French," said the amused voice behind him, and he spun around.

There stood a woman, dressed in Plain clothes, a dark purple cotton day dress, a black apron and black stockings, and shoes. She was wearing a full black bonnet, and David hadn't seen anyone wear one of those for years. His grandmother had worn one, and she had been considered old-fashioned even back then. But then, some of the young ones were re-adopting them.

"Hello!" And then he stopped. Good lord, she was pretty, and pretty women always made him tongue-tied. She even made him light-headed; it was just a flash, and he brushed it off as soon as it happened.

She smiled, and then she was even prettier. "Actually, they're not French; they're Belgians, and they were born in Illinois, so I guess that makes them Yankees."

"I –" He stuttered as he always did around people he wasn't related to. He absolutely didn't know what to say. "I- I- t-this is my barn." It was a lame finish, and he blushed. Fifty years old, and he was blushing like a schoolboy. That just made him blush harder.

She nodded. "Then you are just the person I need to see. Would you mind if I watered the horses from your garden hose? I was hoping to find some water, but no one was around, and there's a lock on the faucet."

Of course, he didn't mind, and that gave David something to focus on other than the pretty woman. He pulled out his keys, walked towards the horses, and they parted for him. Behind the barn were new surprises. A big wagon and three more horses. She hopped up in the wagon and brought back a pile of buckets, and they watered the horses.

"My name's David. This is my f-farm." There, he got that out with reasonable dignity. "D-do you need help? Or were you j-just looking for water?"

"Young Bob threw a shoe, and I needed a place to stop and see what I should do for him, and I thought there might be water around this barn. So it seemed a good place to stop for a minute. I hope you don't mind."

David looked at her. She didn't tell him her name; he didn't miss that. He might be a stutterer, and that made him speak slowly, but he wasn't stupid, no matter what people thought when they heard him.

She'd pulled up behind the barn where she couldn't be seen from the road.

And she was wearing her bonnet wrong.

"No, no – it – it was an emergency. C-can't help that." He looked at the horses. "Which one is Young Bob?"

"This is the poor boy. He's been very patient, considering." She had the missing horseshoe and a hoof knife in the pocket of her apron and pulled them out as she walked over to the horse. Then, as easily as if it was nothing, she nudged the horse, said something David didn't understand, and picked up the hoof, brought it between her legs, and tested the horseshoe on it. Then she stuck the horseshoe back in her pocket and started cleaning and trimming. A farrier had to be strong, and handling a heavy horse meant a lot of skill as well as strength; she was working with the horse one-handed. She knew what she was doing.

She looked up. "I think it just wasn't nailed in properly and worked its way loose. I don't see any splits in the hoof or problems with the shoe. One of those things, I guess." She frowned. "Although I'd like to see a slightly wider shoe on such a big horse, but that's my opinion. I wasn't around when these horses were shod."

She had a slight accent. It wasn't Deutsch. David knew Mennonite accents.

"It's hard to get the oversized shoes. Y-you might have to have them custom forged." David watched her clean and trim the hoof, which she did in a few strokes of the knife. "N-not many people have heavy-y horses now. I d-don't know of any around here." He looked at her. "No one, in fact."

She paused, just for a second, and then pointed to a bag. "I shouldn't have started so fast, but once I get started – Could you please hand me my mallet? It's in the bag." He fetched the mallet, and she pulled out some nails from her apron and replaced the horseshoe. It only took a few minutes.

When she was done, she gently released Young Bob and gave him a pat, and out of the pocket came an apple.

"Thanks for the water and letting me stop here. I really appreciate it. If you don't mind, I'll stay here for lunch and check the hooves of the rest of 'em."

"You're welcome. N-no problem at all. Stay as long as you need to." He gave Young Bob a friendly pat on the rump. "Give the horses a rest. Where're you heading to?"

She walked around and picked up Young Bob's other foreleg, and David felt the massive horse shift his weight. For a minute, he thought she hadn't heard him, but she had. It just took her a long time to answer.

"North."

"An interesting way to t-travel. Wouldn't a car be faster?"

She chuckled but didn't look up. "I don't know how to drive. I can change a horseshoe, but I certainly don't know how to change a tyre."

"Oh, you seem pretty c-capable. I bet you could learn to drive. If you c-can change a horseshoe, you can change a tyre. All the English learn to drive."

Now she really laughed. "I'm not English!"

David grinned at her. "Oh yes, you are. You sure ain't Mennonite."

The smile left her face as fast as a thunderclap, and David was immediately sorry he said anything. He didn't mean to upset her, but she was faking being Old Order, or maybe a recent convert, and he hoped the subterfuge was just for fun or faith, not because she was hiding from something.

"I guess I couldn't fool you, David." She bent back down to the hoof, but it was fine.

"I was born Old Order, very c-conservative. Met a girl who was Anabaptist and didn't want to live in 1860 but was a good woman, so I left and became a bit more worldly."

She moved to the hind legs and examined another hoof. He watched her.

"So, are you running *to* something or *from* something?" She paused, just like before, just for a second.

"Both. It was time for me to leave, and I don't want to talk about why, David." She stood up and looked at him, her face impassive. "I didn't do anything wrong, and everything I own I paid for, so I'm not doing anything illegal. But I have people looking for me, and living off the grid keeps me safe. I would be forever grateful if you didn't talk about me to anyone."

David nodded and tried to smile reassuringly. "I won't t-tell a soul. I promise. You stay here as long as you want; no one will bother you. The road is pretty deserted most of the time." He took a step back from the horse. "Listen, I have a fence gate to finish up before it gets dark. Then I was planning on going to the grocery store. Do you need anything?"

She smiled and shook her head. "Thanks, David. I'm fine. I'm sure your wife is expecting you for dinner, so don't worry about bringing me anything."

"My w-wife had a heart attack and has been g-gone for two years now." He turned and walked away, then turned back and grinned. "She'd tell you to wear the bonnet back on your head more. It's too far forward, and the women would show off a bit of hair in front. And they don't tie it unless it's windy. "

Then he left.

The Fortuneteller

The Fortuneteller believed David. He wasn't lying to her when he promised he wouldn't talk about her, and that gave her the comfort to spend the night behind his barn.

His future was calm, too. When she read his path, she didn't see any upset or danger; in fact, she saw a long, happy life and soon a new romance. But the intertwining paths meant love wouldn't happen until after she was gone. All she knew was that his new, and his last, wife would have blue eyes and her name was Hanna. That made the Fortuneteller cheerful; he seemed like a nice guy, and she loved a happy ending.

She carefully examined all twenty hooves for loose nails, and when that was done, she started a little fire and made herself a cup of tea. She told the horses to stay out of the road and behind the barn so passersby wouldn't see them, but no one drove past. Like David said, the road was very quiet.

It was a surprise, then, when he came back. She was just thinking about dinner when he walked around the corner of the barn, grinning and holding up a bucket of KFC and a six-pack of beer.

"Hi! I'm glad you're still here! I was afraid you'd run off, and then I'd be stuck eating all of this chicken by myself!" He was so delighted to see her that the Fortuneteller had to smile back, and she ran to the caravan to get some knives and forks and a camp stool, but he just waved the stool away and sat on the ground with her.

He had bought her some groceries, too, for the road, he said. Fresh things like milk, bread, and fruit. It was really very sweet of him, and the Fortuneteller was touched. Of course, he wouldn't take any money, and she didn't press him too hard because that would have been insulting, but she couldn't remember the last time a man brought her food. A hundred years ago? Two hundred? Never?

Even Dobil never brought her food, and he was responsible for her.

But then –

They sat on the grass in front of the small fire and shared the beer and chicken and talked, mostly about horses because that topic seemed safe to both of them. Then, as the shadows grew long, he told her about his family. He had six children, all grown up and married, and fifteen (!) grandchildren. Some of them were back in Old Order congregations, and others had followed a more modern path. But all were married and seemed to be doing well. Only one couple wanted to stay with farming, and soon he'd move into town and let them take over this farm and live in the main house. A big house like that needed a family in it, not an old man rattling around by himself.

"I don't think you're old!" The Fortuneteller frowned and gave him a good look. "How old are you? Forty-five? Fifty?" He wasn't a bad-looking guy, not at all, and then it hit the Fortuneteller that he was talking with her like she was a normal woman. A woman he found attractive. That never happened either. Ever.

David laughed. “Close, and thanks f-for that flattering assessment! I’m a few weeks away from the big six-oh. Farming’s hard work, so I g-get my exercise. Maybe that helps.”

She smiled and nodded. Maybe it was the nod that loosened her bonnet. A sudden gust of wind came from nowhere, and the bonnet flew off into the cornfield, a black swirling disaster made of cotton.

And David saw her ears.

Horrified, the Fortuneteller looked at him and threw her hands up to cover them. She moaned and squeezed her eyes shut, waiting for him to run away, terrified to learn he was eating KFC with a witch.

“No, no, no…” he whispered, and she felt him touch her hands. “Don’t cover them up.”

She couldn’t talk, she couldn’t breathe, and as she felt his rough farmer’s hands stroking her cheek, she kept her eyes squeezed shut. She could smell him. David smelled of grass and rain and rich, good earth. He smelled fertile. Sexy.

“No, don’t worry. Don’t be upset.” And he pulled her into his lap. “It’s okay. They’re beautiful.”

And with that, the Fortuneteller started to cry. David had said her ears were beautiful. That had never happened before either.

“Sshh-shhh –” And he kissed her. Gods help her, she kissed back, and between the tears and the kiss, her damn contacts popped out, and she flamed up. And he didn’t run away. He kept kissing her, and they were rolling around on the ground, and she wanted him. So. Bad.

He knew just what to do. David knew where all the buttons and ties were and how to get past the stockings and underclothes and how to get her to the very edge of orgasm and how to finish her off until they were both panting, shuddering, dripping messes.

He loved her ears, and for the first time in her long, long life, a man in lust kissed them and drove her right off the cliff, and she peaked again.

Then he was done and rolled off of her, and they both lay in the grass, half-naked, panting and holding hands. They looked at the stars and both wondered what the hell had just happened.

"Hon – I –"

"My real name is Aethelind, David. You can call me Lindy for short." She steadied her breathing. "That's my secret name."

"Aethelind. That's a beautiful name." He looked at the stars. There were a million of them out tonight, and they were all smiling at him. "That's a good name for a fairy. Aethelind."

"Not a fairy. A lord to some people. A witch or demon to others."

He turned and looked at Lindy. She was still glowing, but not as bright now. The lovely traces of green fire that danced over her skin were fading away, almost gone. David returned to stare at the stars. He had just made love to one of the magic folk. Then he smiled. She seemed to like it! Not bad for an old guy, he thought.

"A lord. So that's why you're going north. To Canada? To escape?"

"Yeah." And she turned on her side and stroked the side of his face. "I have to go; it's time, and I'm afraid to stay here in the States. I almost didn't get out last time, and I've let it get too late this time."

"You can stay here if you want. I'll –" And she put a finger on his lips, stopping him from talking. He knew what she was going to say before she said it.

"You know I can't. You have a family here, a farm, and the world is turning dangerous for people like me. I can't live here any more. You can't protect me. I'll live a long time if I can get to safety." And then she laughed – a musical, happy laugh. "Besides, you have a wonderful life to stay here for. I wouldn't dream of getting in between you and Hanna."

"Who's Hanna?"

"Someone you need to look for. You can start tomorrow, after I leave. I don't know where she is; all I know is that she is waiting for you, and she will make you very happy, the way you've made me very happy tonight."

David looked at Lindy, and in his heart, he knew she was right to leave. But oh dear God, she was beautiful. He would never forget her; that was a given. How could he forget a night with magic?

She sat up, took his hand, and they went to the caravan where they talked and slept and made love all night.

When dawn broke the next morning, they washed up with the cold water from the garden hose, playing and spraying each other like children. The horses were rounded up, fed and watered, and with every completed morning routine, the Fortuneteller stepped a bit further away and out of David's life.

She put on a clean dress and made breakfast, and while they ate, they talked about her dilemma. Go north-west, a much longer trek, and try to cross the border in the prairie? Or north-east, a shorter route but through the lakes, and go across the bridge at Sault Ste Marie? But if she did, she'd have to go through the American border patrol system, and they were looking for passports, and she didn't have one. A lord was shot while trying that.

David frowned into his coffee. The longer the journey, the more possible dangers she'd face. Better to get to Canada as efficiently and as fast as possible. But she couldn't fly in or take the train, not since Meecham tightened the screws and declared people like Lindy as enemies of the state. Demons from hell that could be shot on sight, no less.

He was just a farmer and a pacifist at that. He couldn't protect her against people with guns. He had no idea how to fight if it came to it.

"Can't you go through on some other photo ID?" And Lindy laughed.

"You can't take a picture of a lord! That's why I don't have a driver's license. No photo! I almost didn't get into the US from Portugal, but I bribed a guy at the American consulate and just squeaked in. But that was in 1947, before computers and biometrics and stuff like that."

"1947!"

"I'm very old, David." She smiled, and her eyes glinted. "Very, very, old."

He didn't ask how old because he had a feeling that it would be another magical thing to wonder at, and it wouldn't help her now. Today's issue was keeping Lindy safe so she could get older.

Then he abruptly stood up. "Lindy, don't leave before I get back. I've got to go to the house; you just wait here for me. I won't be half an hour." And he ran to his truck. "Promise me! You won't go before I get back!"

She promised, and David drove off, leaving her to break camp.

It was longer than half an hour, but he was back, and he ran up to give her a big manila envelope.

"Look, I'm giving you Doris' paperwork to get into Canada. It's her Form 4029 and her birth certificate."

Lindy didn't understand, and David had to explain it to her. Doris, his late wife, was an Anabaptist, in a sect that wasn't as strict as what David grew up in, but still had its quirks, and one was the refusal to have a photo taken for government IDs like passports and driver's licenses. One summer, after things tightened up on the border after the 9/11 bombings, they took a vacation to Canada to visit relatives, and they travelled using Mennonite documents, which didn't have photos. A Form 4029 was all that was needed to prove she was a citizen that and her birth certificate was enough to get her through and back.

"You might be old, Lindy, but you don't look it. Take Doris' paperwork. She's been gone t-two years, but I don't think there's any government record, not even a death certificate. She died at home, and we took care of her funeral and everything ourselves. There's no biometrics, no fingerprints, nothing with a Form 4029. Memorise her details in case someone asks, but if you go dressed in Plain clothes and carry this, you can get through the border controls with no passport. If you mail them back to me when you're done, I'll know you've made it over okay."

He grinned. "And maybe tie your bonnet on. I don't think they'll know Mennonite fashion details."

Then he pressed the envelope into her hands and bent down to kiss her.

"I'm n-not going to hang around; good-byes are sad enough. If you need anything, anything at all, you call me. My n-number is in the envelope." He touched her cheek. "You are so special – you have a good life, Aethelind."

Lindy blinked back tears. "You, too, David. I know you will."

And he got back in the truck and drove off. He didn't look back.

Ten minutes later, the Fortuneteller was gone, too.

The Green Man

Ayu was a lord, but like Neptune, so old he didn't know how old he was. The Earth was 4.5 billion years old, and that was probably a good number to work from. He didn't have a particular talent, but he did have a particular realm, and that was Earth itself. He took care of the Earth and worked hard to keep it in balance, moving water here, making a volcano there, doing things that might seem destructive at the time, but keeping the entire world healthy. Hurricanes were terrible for the mice and wrens caught up in them, but they were an efficient way to redistribute heat, and the water they sucked up from the oceans slaked the thirst of inland deserts and plains. Volcanoes created land and provided minerals, and both huge forces fed life.

He thought he was pretty good at it, this Earth building. It was tiring, and he'd go to sleep for millennia at a time, but he went through many cycles. Each time the Earth would change, grow, die, and then he'd give it some nudges and do some work and take the remnants that survived the last cycle and build on them and make something better.

Look at all of the other planets! His Earth was by far the best that circled Sol, the best in the entire starry neighbourhood. There were other earths out there besides Ayu's, he was sure, because the gods never limited themselves, but as far as Ayu could sense, Earth was alone in its perfection. Earth was life itself, and Ayu, The Green Man, was a gardener of life.

When humans evolved, he took their form, and it certainly worked out for the best as far as he was concerned. When elves and other lords evolved as a gift from the gods, Ayu joined them and became part of the tribe of lords, mostly because he was lonely and they were extremely entertaining. He loved visiting and talking with different lords. They all had unique personalities, and, for the most part, they kept busy with their jobs of keeping balance between tribes, and listening to them talk about it was interesting. If Ayu were a farmer, then the lords were ranchers, managing and herding the livestock made up of elves, humans, orcs, and themselves.

The elves understood his purpose, and while they fed him and took care of him when he was around (and asked), Ayu didn't need them. He'd taken care of himself for untold millennia before the first elf sprang from the soil, and the only thing he found handy was their ability to port him from place to place. He could do a lot of things, but porting wasn't one of them, and when he moved around, it was usually the old-fashioned way, on foot.

Occasionally, he called up a big wind to take him someplace, but then he'd get motion-sick. It was better just to walk. He had the time.

The lords The Green Man talked to didn't know what he did because he wasn't a braggart, but they could sense his power. Managing life was difficult to explain anyway, and he didn't want to become a bore.

The lords had different levels of ability. Some were very weak, almost human. Most had real strength, but their abilities were narrow. Then there were Elementals, who were very strong indeed. A couple of Realm Lords were as strong as Ayu.

Some lords thought they were stronger than Ayu, mistaking his easy-going good humour for weakness. They didn't understand exactly what he did because what he did was subtle yet on such a huge scale. They thought that the flora and fauna of the Earth simply were there, a random, lucky creation that wasn't farmed or managed. They didn't see how rare and beautiful Earth was and what made it habitable, and they didn't know that their home was the work of a thoughtful, sentient being. Gaia certainly didn't.

In the beginning, he loved Gaia. She was clever, heart-stoppingly beautiful, and extremely talented; an Elemental woman of immense magical power. She chased after Ayu, seducing and flattering him, and who wouldn't like that? There was an occasional human lover, but here was a lord who was hot for him, and sex with her was mind-blowing. After millions of years of watching other creatures mate, he now had a mate of his own to bed, and she was really, really good at it.

Ayu fell in deep lust, but love? Not as much as he thought at first. For all his vast age, his interpersonal relations experience was pretty basic, and like many emotional teenagers, he had a hard time telling love and lust apart.

Gaia fell in love with Ayu and, without consulting him at all, bonded. She just assumed that if she bonded with him, he'd bond with her, but that's not how it worked out.

As Gaia grew in skill and authority as Primary Lord, she thought less of The Green Man's abilities and began to get impatient with his work. Wasn't the world perfect as it was? Why was he always fiddling with it? Why did he have to go to far-flung, boring places and push a continent one mile west just when she was about to throw a party? She would ask him to do things like alter the weather when it suited her, not when it was best for the Earth, and then wouldn't drop it when Ayu said no, now was not the right time.

Gaia thought farming was simple, that the Earth managed just fine on its own, that the Green Man's efforts were minuscule, and that the exhaustion he experienced after he worked was wasted effort and frankly over-dramatic. If he came to her house and talked about how difficult it was to keep the Sahara region green, she just changed the subject to something more interesting, like music or her own work.

She was sure she knew better on just about every topic, and while she was sweet about it, there was an edge of condescension to her words. To her and other lords, The Green Man was a simple gardener and, unlike elves, didn't produce anything edible. When they were doing important things like keeping chaos agents like the orcs in check or helping elves work and trade with the humans, Ayu would show up at Gaia's doorstep bone-tired, filthy, sweaty, and give her a rare flower or a pretty rock. It was sweet but really rather childish.

When the lords gathered for a party (and wasn't enjoying life the whole point of existence?), a cleaned up and presentable Ayu was there, escorting Gaia and looking handsome and mixing just like anyone else. They felt his age and certainly felt his power, but a few of the busier Elementals wondered why he didn't help Gaia out more. Gaia's court thought he was a bit lazy. For his part, while Ayu hugely enjoyed talking and learning from the others, he didn't keep up with the news, music, poetry, art, or anything really important. He sat and listened more than he contributed. Gaia was occasionally a bit embarrassed by his lack of sophistication. She loved him, but she didn't respect him.

Her lack of respect and the sense of being taken for granted needled more and more as time went on, and as it became more public, The Green Man began to feel like the boy toy of a celebrity. Mr. Gaia.

He had a fling, a human relationship that lasted no longer than the blink of an eye, and since he wasn't bonded to a solo relationship with anyone, including Gaia, his penis worked just fine with a willing human woman. Gaia found out about it and had a screaming fit. She wasn't going to share what she thought she owned, and the more she screamed, the less Ayu loved her, until he really didn't like her at all. He realised that if he was looking for warmth outside of her bed, maybe he shouldn't be sleeping with her.

She had bonded; he had not, and their relationship was crap. Both had spent their entire lives working to achieve balance in the Earth and in the Tribes, but their own relationship was so far out of balance that it was upside down.

The Green Man went to bed angry. He didn't tell her he was sleeping; he just left. Gaia didn't know his vast age; she'd never asked because his pre-Gaia life wasn't important to her. She just assumed that he was a lord like she was. She didn't know that he would go into hibernation, and in that state his spirit would rest, too, and she wouldn't be able to sense it. She thought he was dead and had a mental breakdown. In her despair and rage, she destroyed almost everything she'd loved and worked for.

While Ayu slept, Gaia destroyed her world, only it wasn't *her* world; it was the gods' world, and when she eliminated herself, she eliminated Balance.

Now, after a short sleep of 3,500 years, he was awake, and everything had changed. Vast areas of the Earth had no elves. There were only a few faint traces of either lords or elves, but he had no idea where they were now, and he couldn't find any to talk to. He woke up in Antarctica, and with no elves to port him, he had to leave the continent the hard way, barely making it to South America. Once there, he spent some time in the forests of Brazil (which needed serious work, but that was for later), but he couldn't find a single lord or elf.

Ayu had no idea what was going on, and he couldn't feel Gaia, much less find her. It was as if she had died. He didn't know that he was on the wrong continent, and no elves had been woken up in South America yet. The few lords who had been there had left.

He was worried about the environment, but he didn't want to start altering this new, stinking Earth without more information about what had happened to his last perfect world. He didn't want to make things worse, and right now, it was pretty bad.

Then, when he was walking on a beach in Guyana, he saw a mermaid and called to her. A sea elf! The first of the elf tribe he had come across. If there were mermaids, then Neptune had to still be around. The Green Man would talk to his brother, the Realm Lord of the Seas. Maybe he knew what the hell had happened.

The Fortuneteller

The Fortuneteller looked at the thin envelope of papers and studied them closely. She understood what David was trying to tell her: to let the bureaucracy assume a lie and use that lie as the key to the border's locked door.

It was risky, very risky. She didn't know if the papers were still valid in Meechum's rapidly changing bureaucracy, but she also understood that these papers were, in a computerised, AI world, a way of being "off the grid". Yes, these sheets of paper were in the vast databases where every human was assigned a number and a file, but the technology gaps that made the papers valuable, the lack of biometrics and photographs, couldn't be overcome by a sophisticated AI. Even AI had to have something to work with, and a false picture was easily figured out. For AI, fake and bad was much better than no picture.

Oh, she wished she could read her own future! Of course, she couldn't because when you knew your own future, you could change it, and then it ceased to exist, and you had no future at all. That was the catch-22 of fortunetelling. Knowing everything that was going to happen before it happened meant the obliteration of paths, and if you knew all the paths, you erased everything.

She sat in the wagon and let the team pull her north, and her mind raced around all of the questions like a mouse trapped in a milk bottle. With the boring tarp still covering the entire wagon and with the Mennonites (while still somewhat exotic to modern people) much more common and accepted than gypsies, no one paid that much attention to her when she stopped for water or to let the horses rest. Onlookers loved the horses, but the Fortuneteller herself wasn't a draw, and most people understood that it was rude to photograph the Amish folk. That lack of attention was good, but it also meant fewer distractions, and she had more time to stew.

Whenever she thought of David, she smiled. Yes, she knew her encounter with him was the perfect one-night stand with the perfect man at the perfect time and that there was no going back and trying to repeat it. Clinging to him would never regain that moment and would just ruin it for both of them, so instead she cherished the memory and the lessons she'd learnt.

If a man could accept and love her for who she was, for even just a few hours, maybe one would come along and love her for longer. Maybe forever. When she'd been the only witch in the world, she'd accepted that she was utterly alone and that men were terrified and repulsed by her. But now she knew that other magic people existed, and that brought a glimmer of hope. David taught her that at least one man in the world thought she was beautiful and rare and worthy. Maybe there would be others. Just one would be a miracle.

The lesson of David meant that she had more to gain from going into Canada than just safety and her life; crossing the border meant there were possible new futures for her. It had taken over four hundred years to meet a David; it might take just as long to have her next encounter. But the difference between BeforeDavid and AfterDavid was that now she had hope for the future, even if she had no idea what her future would bring.

Which would be the best way to cross into Canada was still a toss-up. Northwest or northeast, both had their advantages and perils, and both ended in the same place: Canada and the start of a new life. She had the free will to choose, which was as powerful as fate.

She chose northeast. David gave her a key, and she had trusted him once; and she decided to trust him again. There was really no logical reason to trust him, just faith.

The Fortuneteller smiled. She knew her history, being well-read, and she knew the story of the English king. For want of a nail, the shoe was lost. For want of a shoe, the horse was lost. For want of a horse, the king – and the kingdom – was lost.

She'd found her shoe, she'd shod the horse, and that had led her to David. She would be foolish to ignore a gift from the gods, and David was certainly a gift. So with her free will, she would trust the gods, David, and the papers.

That night, she found a good place to hide just east of Stoughton and studied her maps. It poured rain, but the horses found shelter under some trees; she was cosy in her caravan, and all was good with the world.

Maksym and Darnya

A week on, and Maksym and Darnya still had no clue as to the whereabouts of the Fortuneteller. There wasn't a single byte on the internet regarding a red Gypsy caravan, and as much of a splash as she'd made leaving Chicago, you'd think someone in Wisconsin would notice. Unless she was sitting in a warehouse somewhere, gagged and tied (a possibility), the Fortuneteller would be passing by dozens of people every day. Surely *one* would find her romantic caravan Instagram-worthy.

The elves combed police radio chatter, traffic reports, and WhatsApp comments by truckers (who, as a group, would not shut up – they discussed their fuckin' hangnails, for gods' sakes!).

Again, nothing.

Then Darnya had a genius moment. Instead of combing the ether for photos of the wagon and Gypsy lords, could the elves just look for the horses? Those Belgians were big suckers, and people loved them. They already had good photos of the horses, and weren't each horse's hair colour and patterns as individual as a fingerprint? If the lord sold the horses and the wagon was sitting in a warehouse, that would give them something to work with. A place to start looking afresh.

An hour later, she and Maksym had photos of Hairball and Beauty matched to an Amish (!) wagon selling jam that had pulled into a parking lot at a small dam in Lowell, Wisconsin. They didn't have a good photo of the wagon; it was cut off, and there were trees in front, but the single photo of the horses was pristine. The two horses were at the water's edge on a concrete boat ramp, drinking, with the dam behind them. It was a very pretty shot.

The operatives were only an hour and a half away by car. After some high-fives and happy dancing, they were on their way.

If those horses still belonged to the Fortuneteller, it meant that any day she would start turning north-west and make her way through the huge tracts of national forest and head in the direction of Duluth. There she would skirt the very tip of Lake Superior and then beeline to her chosen crossing point.

The intel elves were convinced she was going due north and would try to cross into Canada from Minnesota. Where exactly, they had no idea. While the border was a Swiss cheese of holes, a person could easily cross if they took a canoe or walked. If she was going to take the wagon and horses, there were only a couple of bridges over the unbroken chain of lakes and rivers that made up the US/Canadian border. The horses could ford some of the rivers, but that wagon would never make it across.

Or maybe it could. Maybe, offered Maksym, the damn thing would turn into a boat. He wouldn't put it past the lord. She'd been full of surprises so far.

Maybe her talent was making things float.

They debated possible crossing points on the entire drive out to the Lowell area. They didn't even consider that the Fortuneteller would turn onto the Upper Michigan Peninsula and brave the border guards at Sault Ste Marie. That would be crazy.

The Fortuneteller

The Fortunteller was camped behind the volunteer fire department for the night. The guys washing down the fire truck were really nice, and when she asked if she and the horses could get somc water from their hose, they were happy to help. One thing led to another, and they said, Yeah, no problem for the Amish woman to camp there overnight on her way to visit relatives 'up north". They even did a little grocery run for her.

So when Darnya walked up, the Fortuneteller was sitting by her campfire, making a nice pot of stew. She was sick to death of fast food, and homemade beef stew – Mmmm.

"Hi, Fortuneteller."

She looked up but didn't stop stirring. There was a barely noticeable flash of green behind the brown contacts.

"Hi, Darnya. What's up?"

Darnya came clean. She was a Ranger, an operative from the Elf Nation sent to find and help rescue lords. She and her partner had been looking for the Fortuneteller since the campgrounds outside of Chicago. She gave the Fortuneteller her business card.

"You have others here? Bring them here. I want to see them."

"Just my partner; we work in twos. Too many people can attract attention." Darnya's face didn't betray it, but she was nervous. She didn't know how angry this lord was going to be, and so far, the Fortuneteller wasn't acting friendly. She sent a text to Maksym.

Maksym was waiting in the car about a block away and was there almost immediately, walking up and then squatting down by the campfire. He smiled and held out his hand. "Hi, my name is Maksym –"

The Fortuneteller didn't move, didn't smile, didn't shake his hand. She kept stirring. He put his hand down and sat back, and let Darnya do the talking.

Darnya started telling the Fortuneteller what they could do, extraction plans, and what would happen after the Fortuneteller was in Canada –

She held up her hand. Enough. And she got up and went to the caravan. The operatives heard some rattling around, and they looked at each other. Maksym shifted and coughed.

She came back with three bowls, three spoons, and a ladle and proceeded to give them each a bowl of the stew, and then she started to eat.

"Do you know how old I am, Darnya? Have your elves told you that?"

"No, ma'am."

"I was born in 1590. I don't know where because I was stolen from my parents when I was eight, old enough to remember my name and that I had good parents who loved me and young enough to forget everything else. I was stolen because my eyes glowed, and the Romani who saw me thought I was a witch who could turn rocks into gold. They didn't love me or adopt me, the Romani; they enslaved me.

In all the years I lived with the Roma, I never met another child stolen by them. So I am doubly unique – the only living example of the Roma slurs every gadji knows and a witch.

I think I'm from Poland, but who knows? The Roma were always travelling."

The Fortuneteller looked into a middle-distance past that Darnya and Maksym couldn't share. Then she shook her head and continued, occasionally taking bites of her stew. There was no point in letting good stew get cold.

"During that time, the witch hunts were sweeping across Europe. Germany was very bad. They'd die down, and then something or someone would see a witch, and there would be mass hysteria. What they now call the madness of crowds."

She paused and stirred the stew, looked at Maksym, and spoke in Ukrainian.

"Do you want to know how many men and women – and children – I've seen burnt to death, Maksym? Hung, drowned, drawn and quartered? How many I watched tortured for entertainment for the mobs? No? I wish I could forget how many. Not a one was a real witch, not like me. They were all innocents. Every single one."

The Fortunteller took a bite of her excellent stew, and her eyes looked at nothing but saw everything. The past was always there if you wanted to look. She shuddered and then continued her story.

"When I was about twenty, with no powers at all and yet cursed with glowing eyes and the witch's stink, I escaped slavery and went to travel with another Roma clan. I was always alone because I always had to make sure I had a way to escape. I had no husband and no children because men were afraid of me. A large Roma clan can offer safety in numbers, but it also attracts attention and can bring danger. Everyone hated the Roma. We were Europe's scapegoats – enslaved, killed, tortured. We stole and cheated the gadji, but how else were we to live? They hated us for who we were, and we lived in the shadows and hated back. Me? I wasn't a blood Roma; anyone could see that. And I was a witch, so although the Roma sheltered me, they were also afraid of me. And for many years, I couldn't help them even if I'd wanted to. I had no power.

So I lived alone on the fringes of a fringe people. Sometimes I had a clan who loved me, and I was able to help them, but eventually I always had to leave. Someone would remember that their grandmother had picked apples with the witch a hundred years ago, and my great age would bring attention to me. I'd fade away to find another clan if I could and live on the fringes of that one for a while.

I lived through and avoided witch hunts, the Beng, gods know how many wars, pogroms, concentration camps, the Nazis, the Communists, two world wars in Europe –" She looked up again, but not at the operatives, but back to that memory playing in the middle distance. "Do you think Meecham is the first to hunt me?"

She sighed. "Since 1590, someone has been actively trying to hunt me down and kill me just for being who I am. Every day of my life brought a new danger. But I came here to America, and here was peace. I could relax and feel safe. But now, after seventy years in Chicago, I'm on the move again."

Another ladle of stew in her bowl, and she gestured to the pot for Maksym and Darnya to take another share. The Fortuneteller was hungry, but it was rude to eat alone.

"So today, coming to my fire and eating my food, I have two very nice, very sincere people from the Elf Nation, who I don't know and have never contacted, offering to protect me. Somehow. And take me. Someplace. I see two humans, not lords, not a witch like me. No elves. Just two human people who say "trust me with your life".

I don't know if I can trust you, yet you ask me to trust my life to you. You hand me a piece of cardboard with Elf Nation written on it as if that is enough. It's not.

I don't know what you can do to protect me – if you can at all. But I do know that I can't afford to protect you, and in this most recent pogrom the Americans have started, by helping me, you are risking yourselves.

So this is what I'm going to do. I'm going to go on my way tomorrow, alone, as I've always done. I don't want visits from either of you. I don't want you to attract any attention to me. I'm going to hope and pray that I read you right, Darnya, and that you won't betray me to the witch hunters. That's why you can leave tonight. I could kill both of you now, but I won't. I don't like killing, I've seen too much of it.

Please go now."

She didn't look up, just kept staring into her bowl.

Maksym looked at Darnya, who had tears running down her face, and she looked at him and nodded.

He leaned down and left a card at her feet. “Fortuneteller, if you need us for anything, here are our phone numbers. Call us anytime. We will respect your wishes; you won’t see us again.”

Then they left.

Darnya and Maksym

They spent the next two hours sitting in their motel room writing reports and sending them up through their secure phones to HQ.

“She’s right, you know.” Darnya lay in bed and stared at the ceiling while Maksym finished up his report. He was a hunt-and-peck typist.

“We forget that these lords have been surviving for years, sometimes hundreds of years, on their own and against the odds. We run up like puppies, expecting them to trust us with their lives, to forget survival tactics perfected over centuries, just because, as she said, I have a business card. The young ones, who have parents who contact the EN, they’re happy to see us, but these old ones – everyone has to come to us on their own terms, by themselves. We think we know the best way, and all they say is, *"You think you can protect me? How many orcs have you killed?*”

She turned to Maksym. “I can’t think of a one *old* lord who just jumped up to one of us humans and said thanks for coming, what took you so long?”

“Lord Jan?”

"Nope. Although he contacted us initially, he had to be convinced by other lords; three of them went to Australia looking for him!"

"Lord Chi? He's probably the only one. Even Lord Berke came to us and tested the waters before he brought the rest of the nomads in."

"I wonder what *the Beng* are. Never heard of that." So he typed in the question, and it came back almost immediately. Fiends. Devils.

"Orcs," said Darnya, and Maksym nodded.

"So the next thing I wonder is how she would kill us. That would be interesting to know. She's never said what her ability is."

"Could be a bluff."

Maksym smiled. "I'm not going to call her bluff. That's Lord Judy's job."

He leaned over and turned off the light, and pulled Darnya close. He didn't feel frisky, and neither did she; tonight's encounter with the Fortuneteller had been depressing, and tomorrow they would need to figure out their next steps after HQ had a chance to digest the reports. There was a lot to think about.

The next morning, the orders came and were unsurprising.

They were to follow at a safe distance. No interaction unless the lord approached or contacted them. In the meantime, RumLot Security would see if a lord was available to talk to her, but suitable lords who could be sent to the wrong side of the US border were all tied up with other duties. The Russian border was heating up.

When the exact location of the border crossing was determined, RumLot Security would be there to assist.

Darnya and Maksym were on their own for now.

The Green Man

It was almost more than he could bear. After an ecstatic reunion, Neptune sat on the beach in Yap and told his brother everything. Every horrible, appalling detail over what had happened in the last 3,500 years since Ayu went to sleep.

It was a long story, but the essentials were depressingly short. Ayu stalked off and went to sleep. Gaia had her epic meltdown and, during the summer solstice, called down the sun and (probably, Neptune could only guess) lost control, and the ensuing explosion killed the vast majority of the lords. The few who were left were almost entirely defenceless against the orcs and rebel humans, and they were killed off almost to the last man and woman.

Almost but not quite.

This genocide left the elves vulnerable, and they were almost eliminated, too. Every single elf left on the surface of the Earth was killed, and the rest were driven into hibernation to wait for better times when the great cycle of life turned, as it always did.

Neptune's mermen, the sea elves, left him in a panic to hide in the depths, and they hibernated like their land cousins, and he was alone. So he slept, too, popping up now and then to look for them and see what was going on with the world. He never found a single one.

For 3,500 years, any new lords who were born were ruthlessly eliminated by orcs and humans, although a handful survived by hiding. The elves and the mermen remained in hibernation.

Neptune took a drink of his lager and looked over at the shaken Ayu, sad but not surprised at his reaction. What could Neptune say? That it all wasn't Ayu's fault? It was, and it wasn't. Gaia was responsible for her own actions, but Ayu knew that he was the inadvertent spark to her flame out, and that was true.

"It's like that time when the meteor killed off the dinosaurs. That wasn't your fault either, but you cleaned up after that mess, and while things looked pretty grim then, it allowed the four tribes to grow, didn't it? Maybe this mess will bring some good." Neptune tried to put a good spin on the disaster, if only to spare Ayu the crushing guilt that his brother could see in his eyes.

Ayu stared into his beer, tears streaming down his cheeks. He'd gone to sleep, and that simple act of neglect had killed all of his old friends except for his brother Neptune. They never knew if they were real biological brothers or not, but it didn't matter; they were brothers growing up, and they were brothers now. The blast would have killed Neptune, too, but he wasn't fond of Gaia and didn't go to her ceremonies.

"If I had just told her I was leaving her instead of running off to sulk –"

"She would have still had a meltdown. She had bonded, and your leaving would have torn her soul in two. You couldn't stay if you weren't part of her, could you? Her grief and her death were inevitable, and it was her own, stupid, arrogant fault."

Neptune took a drink. The Adnams was good and came directly from Southwold, where his elves picked it up by the case. Not everything the humans did in their new, stinking world was bad.

"I know, but maybe I could've managed her better so she didn't take down the entire world with her."

Neptune shrugged. "She didn't take down the entire world, just our part of it. The rest of the world still pushed on, just unbalanced. But Ayu, balance is returning even without you. Maybe the gods thought we weren't on the right path and wanted a clean slate to start over. I wasn't the best of lords to my mer-folk; I see that now. You did good, but maybe could have done better with Gaia – but I doubt it. I never really understood what you saw in her. I thought she was a spoiled snot, and she thought I was a stupid party boy."

He looked at his mer-folk, lounging on the beach. "We were both right."

"Anyway, the lords are coming back. The elves and the mer-folk are coming back. Balance is returning, but it's not going to be easy for us. There are new Primaries, a couple this time, and I think they have the right attitude. You need to go meet them."

"Do you think they'll agree to see me? Gaia's court wasn't – "

"They have no choice. They need every single lord they can find. There aren't many of them, and as Caddy keeps saying, there are three billion humans and orcs on this Earth now. Actually, she undercounts. There are nine billion. This new lord clan can be overwhelmed if the humans put their minds to it."

"Nine billion!"

"Yeah, it's like a jellyfish invasion. Massive overbreeding. They'll implode pretty soon anyway when they strip the Earth of food, but the risk is that they take the lords and the elves down with them again."

Ayu was even more depressed. Nine billion!

"Nine billion is too much for three thousand lords to manage. There will have to be a catastrophe to reduce those numbers. Managed decline will be hard."

Neptune sighed. "I don't think there are two hundred lords in the world now, and that's just a guess. I'm not on land. Caddy has gathered a shade over one hundred. More show up all the time, but not enough."

"One hundred? That's it?" Ayu was physically sick. A breeding population of one hundred was theoretically extinct.

"That's all I know of. Many are children. There are only six of us from what the elves call Before Times. There are nine Elementals, which is a lot out of a hundred, but they all don't know how to use their powers yet. They're not experienced; some are only a century old. There are two Warrior Lords and maybe some more on the way."

"I'm so sorry –" And Ayu started to cry, great sobs ripping from his heart. Neptune cried, too, and put a huge arm around The Green Man and hugged his brother.

"It's not your fault; it's everyone's fault. It's my fault, too. I think the gods saw that we weren't on the right path and gave a good reset. That's what they do, and they've done it before. But you're back now, Ayu! I thought you were dead, too! I can't do the land stuff like you can; I'm the Sea. The humans and orcs are land, but I'll help where I can."

He shuddered and pulled himself together. "They need you, Ayu. You have to go help them. My sea folk need you to clean up Gaia's mess so they can live in safety, too. The orcs and humans are killing the sea, and they'll kill us. They'll starve us out."

Ayu nodded. Of course, he had to go and restore balance. He had no choice; it was what he did. But nine billion humans and orcs! They would fight his controlled decline to reasonable numbers because that's what living things did. They only wanted to reproduce; it was in their essence to have children and increase their numbers. But like an algae bloom or an infestation of lemmings, they would outstrip their resources and die off anyway if they weren't managed.

He would go to these new Primaries, a couple who shared the job and the power, unlike Gaia, who had hoarded it all. Neptune liked them, and it seemed that he was a pretty good judge of character for an old fish.

In the meantime, he and his brother got roaring drunk on the good Suffolk lager and talked and cried and reunited all night.

Darnya and Maksym

Two days later, to Makysm's and Darnya's and all the elves' great astonishment, the Fortuneteller was still heading due north.

"Maybe," mused Darnya, "she's going to avoid Minneapolis from the north. We all assume she'll go south, but there are lots of huge parks and forests to the north near the lake."

Every day, either Darnya or Maksym would drive past her and physically locate the Fortuneteller and send a Situation Report to HQ. They were sure she recognised the cars; how could she not? The routes she chose were tiny and very empty rural American backroads, and the few cars that passed her would be noted. When the same make and model pass by three times a day, it would be hard to ignore. But she never waved, looked up, or acknowledged them at all, and they never signalled back. Both sides pretended the other didn't exist.

The operatives leapfrogged around the slow-moving caravan, and at night, when the Fortuneteller was camping in some quiet, deserted place, the Darnya and Maksym found a nearby motel and stayed there. The next morning, they'd track the lord down, and the entire dance would start again.

The Fortuneteller spent the night in the Waupaca County Forest, a little recreation area where she found a couple of ponds and could water the horses. The next morning, she didn't go up a tiny side road west towards Waupaca but instead went east and for the first time followed a four-lane interstate north. It took them an hour of backtracking to find her, even with two cars covering the area, but once they hit I-10, there the Fortunteller was, slowly riding up the interstate on the berm, trucks and cars whizzing past her at seventy.

At the first exit over Walla Walla Creek, she turned east, back onto the farm roads. When they saw her going towards Weyaweaga, Darnya predicted Hwy X (Wisconsin had a weird road-naming system) to New London, and she was right. If the Fortuneteller had heard them talking about routes and predicting possibilities, she would have laughed. They were telling her fortune! They were looking at the possible paths and predicting outcomes. She would have thought, "Not bad for rank amateurs! But predicting the next few days is child's play. Show me what you can do for the months or years ahead!"

Maksym and Darnya began to plan for the worst. The Fortuneteller was either going to some secret crossing that would take her across Lake Superior, or she was going to cross at the international border in Sault Ste Marie.

Maybe she had hired a boat? A ferry? They could lose her if she crossed the lake, but at least on the other side, she'd be in Canada.

Darnya didn't think she'd abandon the caravan and the horses. Giving up her only means of transportation, as well as her home on wheels, would go against hundreds of years of training. But how was she going to get five horses across Lake Superior? The herd weighed over three tons all by themselves. She wasn't going to do it in a canoe.

The operatives speculated, talked with the elves in HQ, consulted with General Jameson, and drove on.

Maksym, Darnya, and The Fortuneteller

In this part of Wisconsin, the retreating glaciers of the last ice age did two things. They either gouged out holes that became lakes or they sanded down the land so that it was pancake flat. There was no "up" in good parts of Wisconsin, but there was a lot of "down". The human-made roads tended to be ruler-straight and meet at right angles except when they had to avoid one of the hundreds of lakes, ponds, or rivers. Part of the Fortuneteller's map work every night was figuring out the most efficient route that followed the farm roads and had a camping place, like a park, all the while working her way around obstacles like big towns, interstates, two-lane highways, and lakes. So it was a constant zig-zag as she headed north, and when the obstacles were taken into account, she didn't always have many options.

Maksym and Darnya became pretty good at figuring out the next campsite once they decoded the lord's criteria.

So when they got the call from the Fortuneteller telling them she was in trouble and needed help, they knew exactly where to find her. She'd stopped overnight at a wildlife preserve, the Navarino Nature Center.

It was one in the morning, and it took them a good forty minutes to throw on some clothes and get there from Gillette, where they had checked into a motel. The Fortuneteller didn't say what was wrong; she was only on the phone for the briefest of seconds.

"Darnya? Can you and Maksym come to me? I'm at the Navarino Nature Center. I need help." And she hung up.

They didn't even know she had a phone on her, but once she made the call, Darnya had her number, and, of course, that was uploaded to HQ. As Maksym drove, Darnya checked their weapons, and the elves in Lowestoft scanned for any police communications traffic in the area that the operatives needed to know about. The emergency comms were quiet, but whatever had made the lord call for help must be serious. She wouldn't call unless it was.

As they turned into the center's long driveway, they switched off their headlights. Maksym left the car, and Darnya drove the last hundred yards, alert for any trouble. As soon as she made it to the center's main parking lot, a shadow emerged and waved her to stop. It was the Fortuneteller.

"Don't come any closer. I don't know if this place has security cameras. Thanks for coming, Darnya. Where's Maksym?"

"He's coming up on foot. To cover me in case I'm walking into something. What happened?"

"I killed a beng, and I need you to dispose of the body."

Darnya blinked.

"Ooo-kayyy –"

And the Fortuneteller told her the story.

She had turned up the road to the nature center, and everything had seemed fine. There were a couple of cars in the parking lot, hikers and picnickers, and one car followed her in. She went inside and did her little play-acting bit. "I'm a wandering Mennonite going to visit people up north. May I water my horses in your pond?" Of course, they said yes.

Then, when they were all outside admiring the Belgians, one of the guides objected. He wasn't too happy with the big horses disturbing the reeds at the pond's edge, so there was a bit of to and fro while the employees discussed the best place for the horses to drink. But they were a nature center, and horses were nature, and they weren't going to stress the animals if they could help it. In the end, the manager gave the Fortuneteller the garden hose and the key to the shed where the faucet was, and she watered the horses that way. It was after five, and the center employees wanted to go home, so the Fortuneteller was told to put the key in the mail slot when she was done with the hose, and the staff left.

No one noticed the man in the parking lot, slumped down in the blue car, listening to everything.

By six, the parking lot was empty except for the blue car, but it was empty, too, and the Fortuneteller didn't worry about it. She pulled her wagon down a side trail in case security cameras were watching the parking lot, so anyone looking would think she had left. Then she set up camp. The odds were that no one actively watched their security cameras at all; they only looked at them later if there was an incident.

Right after midnight, the horses neighed a warning that someone was in her camp. Afraid that an intruder was going to hurt or steal her horses, she dressed and opened the door, and there he was, the man from the blue car – a beng. She could smell him.

The devil-man pointed a gun at her and told her to step down.

He didn't smell her, so he didn't rush her; he was taking things slow, enjoying himself. He wasn't there to rob; he was there to rape.

A little Amish woman. I've never had one of you before. You're number twenty-three, he said. The Fortuneteller could smell him because the night breeze was blowing right at her, and oh stars, he was so rank. He laughed. She would be easy! She was all alone, no weapons – because the Amish didn't carry weapons, do they?

He asked her if she was scared. He wanted her to be scared.

He reached out to touch her, the gun cocked. Don't move. I'll shoot. I don't care if you're alive or dead when I fuck you –

So she killed him.

By the time she got to that part of the story, the Fortuneteller, Maksym, and Darnya were all standing next to the body, lying next to the caravan's door, just where he'd fallen.

"So, as you can see, now I have a problem. I can't call the police. I can't leave him here to be found, not if I'm on the center's security camera. They'll look at the last twenty-four hours if they find a body here. I can't bury him here without the park people noticing a disturbance. His car is in the parking lot. If it's abandoned there, that will get the employees worked up, looking at camera footage, and asking questions. They'll think he's lost in the park."

She sighed. "I could put him in the back of the caravan and just take him with me until I find a good dumping place – it won't be the first time – but there's still the car and camera problem. I don't drive. If I'm stopped by the police as one of the last people to see him, I'll have a hard time explaining away a dead body. Besides – he stinks."

Darnya nodded. The Fortuneteller had thought everything through, followed all the possibilities.

"If you don't mind me asking, how did you kill him?" Maksym looked at the orc with professional interest. There wasn't a mark on him.

The Fortuneteller gave the body a nudge with her foot. "He's not dead, not totally. His heart has stopped, but he's not dead. They come back, y'know. The beng are tough, and they come back from what would kill a human. That's probably where the myth of zombies comes from. I tore an artery, the one in his neck. He'll have a bit of brain damage when it heals and he wakes up, but that won't change his quality of life. He's a beng. His brain doesn't work right anyway."

Darnya looked at the man and then at the Fortuneteller. No wonder she wasn't afraid of sleeping alone in a wooden caravan! All she had to do was look at an attacker and with her magic tear something internally. She wondered how the lord had figured that out by herself. The first time must have been terrifying.

She would have to tell Victor; he'd find this interesting. The very strong lords didn't bother with such subtle defences, and it obviously had never occurred to them to do that when they could just annihilate an opponent. The weaker lords weren't trained to use their baby skills at moving things to mess up the innards of an attacker. She supposed moving an artery a few inches until it tore was no different from moving a plate or a salt shaker down the dinner table.

Well, the lord commanded, and like the elves, the human operatives obeyed. They had to get rid of this orc, and that's what they were trained to do, so they got to work. The orc was tied up, gagged (even though he was totally out, but as the Fortuneteller said, he could wake up), and thrown in the trunk of Maksym's car. By then, he had already called up HQ about their rubbish problem. They told him to drive to International Falls, where a human RumLot team would hop the border and take the orc back to Canada, where he wouldn't be Maksym's problem any more. They had ways.

Darnya took the keys off the orc and, after putting a disposable clean suit on (the Fortuneteller was fascinated by the kit they had in the trunk of their car, the full secret agent array), she drove the orc's car about two miles away and abandoned it deep in some bushes. If no one was looking, it wouldn't be found for weeks, if not months. Maybe forever. Darnya was pretty sure the orc hadn't told anyone what he was doing that evening or where he was going. It would take a while before anyone started searching for him, and in the meantime, the Fortuneteller would be long gone.

The elves in Ukraine were already working on erasing all evidence of the lord and operatives from the security camera's backup servers.

Maksym tracked his partner, and as soon as she left the orc's car, he was there to pick her up.

As they pulled away, her phone pinged a message. Maksym got his at the same time.

"Thank you. – Lindy"

A half hour later, Darnya was in the motel room, writing her report, and Maksym was on his way to International Falls, a seven-hour drive. He hoped the orc wouldn't wake up before they got there. If the goon shit or peed in the trunk, he'd have to clean it up.

The Green Man

He didn't know how long he was with Neptune, probably just a couple of days. After Ayu and Neptune's drunken reunion, there was a period of sleeping off their mutual hangovers, and then a day of talking and re-bonding, and then another day of feasting and drinking with the mer-folk and a brand-new hangover to enjoy.

Then the mermen ported his rather ragged, hungover ass to Lowestoft, where they shoved Ayu very unceremoniously onto the beach under the Claremont Pier and gave him directions to go to The Rum Lot shop.

"The elves tell us it's just a block away, whatever that is, and you'll see a sign."

Five minutes later, Ayu was standing naked (it never occurred to either him or the mer-folk that he should find some clothes to put on) and bleary-eyed in front of the till in the Christmas bauble shop, much to the amusement of the elves and to the surprise of the customers, who were there to buy balls and decorative dangly things, just not those kind. They certainly weren't expecting to see a tall, well-built, naked, sea-weedy lord wander in, complete with huge elf ears that towered over his head and dripping white hair that rippled down to his waist. Or almost white hair. There was a lot of seaweed in it.

Ayu was hustled to the back, given some swim trunks to put on that they kept for Neptune, and he was ported to Aelfeham House.

Darnya

Darnya slept in. Around ten, right on time, Maksym messaged her that he was done, no problems delivering his package, and he was going to catch some sleep and then come back tomorrow, but in a different car. Should be there about lunchtime.

That settled, she went out to breakfast and stopped at a Walmart and bought some doughnuts, some fresh groceries, and a bag of apples for the horses. Then she went out to track down the Fortuneteller, AKA Lindy.

Since they were on a first-name basis now, and since she had her phone number, Darnya thought she'd take the risk and see if she could build on that. If Lindy told her to back off again, she would.

If you can't call a girlfriend to dispose of a would-be rapist's dead body, who can you call?

She kept the motel room by Gillette and looked at her maps and decided that a day's walk for the horses would put them close to nearby Christie Lake. The north side had a boat ramp and would be very private. Just the thing.

When the shadows started to get long she hopped in the car and drove down Country Road V and passed the caravan on the first try; it was only a couple of miles from the Christie Lake access road. Darnya loved it when she was right.

She considered pulling off on the side of the road by the ramp entrance, but decided that would look weird sitting on the verge out here in the middle of God's Country, so she turned into the access gate and drove down the long, dirt road to the ramp.

Half an hour later, the caravan pulled in, too.

The Fortuneteller didn't look surprised when she hopped off the wagon, but Darnya was sure there was an eye roll.

But she smiled and waved and walked over to Darnya's car.

"Hi! I –"

Darnya jumped in. "If you want me to go, just tell me, and I'll leave right now. But I thought I'd check on you, and this place is very private."

The Fortuneteller nodded and shrugged. "It's private to us, I guess. But if you don't mind leaving –"

"Okay. No problem"

" – after dinner, that would make me feel better."

Darnya relaxed and grinned. The Fortuneteller was going to be okay.

They unhitched the horses and took them down to the boat ramp one by one and let them have a good drink. After rubbing the horses down, the Fortuneteller and Darnya let them go graze on what grass they could find under the trees. It wasn't until the horses were happy that dinner could be started for the two women.

During dinner (sandwiches made from the fresh groceries Darnya bought), Darnya told Lindy (she was allowed to use that name now) what had happened with Maksym and the orc.

The orc didn't wake up during the transfer, which was good, and the RumLot people smuggled him to Canada in a canoe (which we can do for you, Darnya pointed out, but Lindy shook her head. The horses and caravan were coming with her, and neither would fit in a fleet of canoes). Once in Canada, the orc was given to the local elves, who found out very quickly that he was a serial rapist the Wisconsin police had been trying to find for years. So they decapitated him and buried the bits so deep it would take a coal miner to find them.

"Elves really don't like orcs. It would have been hard to stop them from finishing the job even if we wanted to. And turning him over to the Canadian police would just have complicated things."

Sitting cross-legged by the tiny campfire, Darnya ate her sandwich and looked at the lord, wondering how hard she could push her.

"So, how do you plan to get across the border? From what we see, you're going to be stopped by Lake Superior pretty soon in the east, and crossing from northern Minnesota means nothing but rivers and lakes that way, too. Like you say, the horses and the caravan won't fit in a canoe – or even a houseboat."

Lindy looked at Darnya and then shrugged. In for a penny, in for a pound, and the RumLot couple had proven their worth. "Sault Ste Marie. It's a lot closer, and I'm going through the normal passport gates. I have a golden ticket."

Darnya frowned. Lords didn't always know how the modern world worked. They were so old, and some were so isolated that they had big gaps in their knowledge.

"You'll need a passport or some photo ID, or other official documentation now. You'll have to have a valid passport to get through the American side, to prove you're not a lord, and then a valid passport or NEXUS card to get into Canada. Although we can easily manage that, it's the Americans we have to worry about. It's not like it was before Meechum. And you can't fake it. Everything is on international databases now."

"Can your RumLot people check the databases?"

Darnya nodded. "They can do miracles. What do you need to know?"

Lindy went to the caravan and came back with David's envelope.

"A friend gave me his late wife's documents. Could your people check these and see if they'll work?"

Darnya looked at the papers. She had never heard of a Form 4029 before and took a photo of both the Form and the birth certificate.

"Dinner's over, and I don't want to have to use my headlights to get out, so I'll go now. Maksym should be back around lunchtime, and we'll see if we can find you. Maybe I'll have some news about this paperwork. If it won't work, you'll have time to think about alternatives. You call me if any orcs come and bother you again!"

"I'm not worried about you finding me, whether I want to be found or not."

Darnya wasn't quite sure how to take that, but she just smiled and shrugged. "Keeping lords safe is my job."

And with that, Darnya left.

Caddy, Kyrylo, and The Green Man

Caddy didn't know what to do with this new lord, Ayu, and she proceeded cautiously. The elves told her and Kyrylo during the briefing that he was a Neptune, a realm lord of such huge power and age that his limits were unknown, but not a god – not yet, at least.

He was Gaia's man, the man she went insane over.

If he challenged her and Kyrylo, there wasn't much they could do. From the elves' point of view (without saying so to her directly), they would follow him if he ordered it. If he took Caddy and Kyrylo's place as Primary, the best they could hope for would be to try to guide him in this new world and be grateful if he took advice. He would have no clue at all what the modern world was like and the dangers posed by the technologically advanced humans.

Kyrylo was especially nervous, although from the outside he was calm. Caddy could tell from the way he drummed his fingers on the arm of his chair. If this lord told the elves to dump all the modern stuff and arm up with horses and swords, they would do it, unquestioningly. If he were angry with humans, he could dismiss the entire human army Kyrylo had so carefully built up. Kyrylo wouldn't be able to reform them under his own banner without the financial assistance of the elves, but that could stop if the elves thought that would go against their new master. He would certainly never use his own army against the elves.

When they asked the elves what exactly his power was, they were vague. An old, old woman who had met him before said, "He's the opposite of Neptune. Neptune is Lord of the Sea, and Ayu is Lord of the Land. He wants things to live, so he changes the land to make everything fertile for us to grow on and for the animals and plants to live on. He uses weather, fire, earthquakes, snow – all that stuff to alter the environment. He's The Green Man. He creates life."

"He creates life." All Caddy could do was look at Kyrylo in wonder. The Green Man. Both primaries were now well-read in folklore and myths, always looking for clues in the Before Times past that would guide them with the elves and lords. The Green Man was in every single human tribe's mythology in one form or another. He had many names, and the details changed, but everyone from Aztecs to Greeks to Celts to Ainu agreed on one thing. He was powerful, and he created life and the setting for living things to flourish.

They had fifteen minutes to absorb the briefing, and Lord Ayu would be there. They would just have to deal with whatever happened. He was being cleaned up now, and the elves had given him a bite to eat so he wouldn't come to them famished and cranky.

The lord was hungover from partying with Neptune, a detail that made Caddy sigh. Figures.

When the door opened to the grand meeting room at the London embassy, Caddy and Kyrylo weren't ready, but as Kyrylo said later, they never would be. Lord Ayu walked in dressed in a navy blue EN uniform. On his shoulders were the epaulettes of an Elemental. Embroidered on them was a full moon. Just like Caddy and Kyrylo wore.

He was tallish, about Kyrylo's height but maybe an inch taller, with the huge ears and the stark white hair of a fully ripened lord with a long braid that went down his back. His eyes were blazing blue. He was, by any human standard, a handsome man, but not pretty. He walked up to Caddy and held out his huge hand, and his eyes crinkled into a smile. "I was told five minutes ago this is your greeting, to shake hands. I hope I'm doing it right. My name is Lord Ayu, and I'm very happy to meet you." Then he turned to Kyrylo and shook his hand, and they sat down and went from there.

Lord Ayu was charming – a really, really nice guy. He listened more than he talked and seemed to sincerely want to know what was going on in this new world. When he talked about the disaster and how he'd slept through it, both Primaries could see how upset he was. He was stunned, almost speechless, and the guilt over his role played across his face in waves of blue fire as he spoke.

He didn't want any leadership role with the elves and the lords; he said he was going to be too busy fixing the Earth.

"Even before, I didn't do anything much with the lords; that was Gaia's job. She didn't understand my work; sometimes I think she didn't want to. I know she found it boring and inconvenient, but I had to do it anyway. That's what I'll do now, bring the world back to health. I've done it before."

Kyrylo asked what he'd done before. Were there other balance catastrophes?

"Oh yeah. When that meteor hit, it took me millennia to make things right again. I thought the dinosaurs were a pretty big accomplishment, but they were gone in a generation, and all that was left were birds. But it worked out okay in the end. That's when humans and lords and elves started to emerge, and that's when I morphed into my present form. I planted a few seeds, nudged a bit here and there, and made some temperature adjustments back and forth. Ice ages are very useful. I was happy with the results."

Caddy just stared. This lord was old when dinosaurs walked the Earth. He was here when the Chicxulub Impactor hit. Neptune probably slept through that one, too.

Ice ages are very useful. I was happy with the results. Ayu was a shaper of worlds. A farmer on a cosmic scale.

"Do you think we can achieve balance again?"

Ayu was startled at the question. "Of course! Balance will always be achieved. We couldn't stop it if we wanted to. *I* can't stop it. The question is how long it will take and how traumatic the shift will be. Neptune told me there are nine billion humans on the Earth now and only about a hundred lords. That's a very, very poor ratio. I'll work to control and reduce the number of humans and orcs, but constant natural disasters are a crude way to do it and can cause as many problems as they solve. I'll have to think about this. Study the lay of the land, think about the consequences of everything I do, and try not to make the situation worse."

The Green Man looked at the primaries, two rather ordinary-looking people with a huge job. But they had started with nothing, and they were working hard to bring balance back against a tidal wave of humanity. He didn't underestimate them, and he wouldn't undercut their efforts as long as they all worked for the same goal.

"I was told by the elves when I was getting the seaweed cleaned off that you have a place, a house where the lords live, and that I could rest there and study the world. I could learn what has changed and what these new humans can do. They said I could come and go as I pleased while I work. Could I ask for shelter from you, to live in your house while I study? If not, I understand, and I'll find someplace else. But as long as you work towards regaining proper balance, I'd like to work with you, and if I'm close by, it'll make things easier."

Caddy was so relieved, she was in tears. Kyrylo let out a big shuddering sigh. Of course, Ayu could stay at Aelfeham House while he studied the Earth's biosphere and environment. As long as he wanted.

RumLot Security

The elves were intrigued by the Form 4029. They started secretly watching the computers at all of the US border crossing points to see how they worked when someone else presented one, and they were a bit surprised at the number of Anabaptists, Mennonites, and all of the various sects who used the form as their passport. No one in RumLot Security knew that the churches had set up missions all over the world, and the young people who couldn't afford to buy land in the US had emigrated to more financially prudent areas. Quite a few had emigrated to South America, and they would fly back to the US to visit relatives, trade, and for all the normal reasons any other person would.

They looked into the birth certificate and cross-checked to see if Doris' death would trigger any alarms, but since it was unregistered, it didn't. As far as the US government was concerned, Doris was still alive, the papers were still valid, and if she wanted to go to Canada to visit relatives, there was no reason to stop her.

There were no red flags, and if that was the way the lord wanted to enter Canada, the EN would work on their end to make the crossing as safe as possible. As Lord Aethelind made her way east, they put their own plans in place.

She was ten days away.

They told her about the extra undercover security that would be blanketing the area just for her. It all seemed a bit over the top, and Lindy started feeling very guilty at the fuss everyone was making – and flattered at the same time. Everyone was determined to get her over the border safely.

On day five, they were only one hundred and twenty-two miles from the border, and Lindy asked Darnya and Maksym if the elves could arrange a horse truck and a flatbed to take the horses and caravan over the bridge. She'd been on her phone studying the bridge crossing itself, a very high, very busy, older two-lane road, and she was concerned about the horses pulling the caravan up that slope for so long. She was also worried that the police would decide she was a nuisance and stop her, although Mennonites could pretty much travel where they wanted.

"I can hitch another two and drive the caravan as a four-in-hand. Going up steep hills is why I bought four horses in the first place, but it's still asking a lot of them. Four were for big hills, and I liked Beauty, so I just bought her anyway and told myself she was my insurance."

Darnya had brought some pizza, and they were eating dinner around the campfire. Lindy seemed really embarrassed to be asking for help again; it made Maksym smile. She had no idea how valuable every lord was to the EN.

"I have the money. If you guys can arrange enough horse trailers and a flatbed, they can go over first, and I'll sit in the back of your car and go over with you. It might be more low-key than me blocking traffic on that two-lane for gods know how long. There's a centre barrier; no one would be able to pass me, and that will draw a lot of attention to me."

If Lindy could hear it, the sighs of relief on two continents would have blown her pointy ears off.

The elves did their computer magic, and all of the vet's documents and animal import paperwork were updated, and everything was put in place. They would stay camped in place until the trucks came in to pick up the horses and the caravan. Then she'd ride with Maksym and Darnya to the border, only about an hour and a half away by car.

The Green Man

When Ayu walked into Aelfeham House, there was no doubt that *this* lord was going to be properly taken care of. Since the Freyja debacle, Caddy had reorganised the structure for managing the lords so that there was enough redundancy in the system that no newbie would ever fall through the cracks again (she hoped). Jack and Alizah still had their duties guiding and mentoring, but with a baby on the way, Alizah would need some recovery time after the birth, and both would need time to take care of the baby. Elves could do a lot of nanny work, but they'd never replace a parent.

Rita and Köke were the new Aelfeham House management team. When Köke finished up his Warrior Lord training, he would be in charge of the security for the area. With his centuries as Berke's number two over the nomads, he'd had plenty of experience dealing with lords living together in a tight group. Two lords fighting over a woman wouldn't bother him at all.

Rita didn't have Köke's experience as a leader, but she was quite good at dealing with diverse personalities, and she was very happy to have a real job she could grow into. Caddy wanted someone there all the time – not only for new lords but also for lords who weren't adjusting well, because she didn't want another Gary either. He should have been under a counsellor's care as soon as people noticed him hiding in his room.

So Ayu was treated like royalty with someone to take him to every meeting or meal, people to always chat with, and everyone happily answering any question he had. While no one knew exactly what he did or how he did it, wearing the blue uniform from day one with the full moons made the lords in the Breakfast Room sit up and take notice. Many years later, he told Caddy that he'd had no idea what the moons meant and hadn't paid any attention to things like rank. He'd just thought everyone was really nice.

It certainly was a change from his position in Gaia's court, where he'd been tolerated only because he shared Gaia's bed. Once different Elementals and courtiers discovered he had absolutely no influence on her official decisions, he was ignored even more. If one of Gaia's sycophants didn't talk to him, that didn't bother Ayu in the least bit, especially when Gaia was chasing after him in those heady days of their fresh romance. But when the lords of Aelfeham House made a point of inviting him to a card game, or asked him to sit down with them for a meal, or even just asked how his day went, Ayu realised just how disdainfully he was treated.

During vast periods of time, Ayu was alone, working, and having friends wasn't possible. When something just isn't possible, you don't worry about it, or you go insane. He had Neptune to visit when neither was busy with their own realms, which wasn't often. When the humans, orcs, lords, and elves appeared, it took a very long time for each tribe to evolve to the point where an individual could have interesting conversations, more interesting than, say, talking to a velociraptor or a hyena. Orcs never did evolve.

Humans and orcs lived tiny lives, so it wasn't worthwhile making long-term friends with them. Lords and elves were much better, and both developed complex societies, so when Ayu took the form of the Green Man, he started to make friends. He even found a few lovers, but his ingrained shyness that came from living alone for millennia kept his social circle very, very small, which meant he really didn't know how to act around people. Not to mention, he was busy. There was always something that needed fixing or improving on his Earth, and he never neglected her.

But this group wouldn't let him quietly sit and watch from the sidelines. They weren't interested in his famous girlfriend; they were interested in him. That was new.

One of the first people Ayu met was Adem, and when he told Adem he remembered him performing at parties and how much he admired his playing, Adem blushed so hard Malachi thought he was going to need sunscreen. They sat down and talked about music for almost two hours. Actually, Adem did most of the talking, with Ayu asking an occasional question or offering a little story or memory of long-forgotten parties. By the time Adem left, Ayu didn't know it, but he had a friend for life. Adem was smitten, the same way he was smitten on his first meeting with Caddy. Not romantically, but he loved Ayu as a new member of his family.

Ayu wasn't required to go to any of the lord classes, but he did anyway. Mostly, he used his time to study modern life, everything from biology to the agricultural policies of various countries to climate change science to human psychology. He loved all of his classes and soaked up information like a sponge.

When you are older than rocks and for untold ages nothing much has changed, learning new things was a joy.

But the biggest difference in his new community was the women. There weren't many unbonded female lords, but between the single lord women of the nomads, the teenage lords just flowering into womanhood, and the human women who worked for the RumLot companies, Ayu found that he was chased by plenty of women who flirted, seduced, and a couple who made pests of themselves over the new *single* full moon Elemental. That was new, too.

When he was with Gaia, no woman ever made a pass at him; they wouldn't dare cross their Primary, and he honestly didn't know that was the reason why a warm smile had never developed into anything else. He understood dominance and social structures in animals. Lords and humans? No.

So that's where the Green Man was when he walked into Aelfeham House. A man of massive talents who didn't think other people were interested in them or in him. A man of ancient age who'd lived alone for so long that he had huge holes when it came to normal social relationships and hierarchies. A man whose fingers were badly burnt by the one woman who'd said she loved him. A woman who, in a fit of petulance, almost destroyed two entire tribes and everything he'd worked so hard for. A man who could shape worlds but didn't understand the new one he was walking into.

Lindy

The hour and a half to the border was the longest hour and a half in the Fortuneteller's long, long life. She hadn't entrusted her safety to someone else since she was a child.

The professional horse hauliers were fine. They had driven all night to get to the Upper Peninsula, but after picking up the load, all they had to do was drive the hour and a half and transfer the horses to another truck in Canada. They were paid very, very well to work fast and keep their mouths shut, and they did both.

The caravan was quickly winched up onto a flatbed tow-truck that was even easier and faster to source, and Maksym and Darnya promised on their honour that both the horses and the caravan would be waiting for Lindy in a RumLot secure warehouse in Sault Ste Marie.

Lindy sat in the backseat of Maksym's car, Darnya riding shotgun, and her white-knuckled hands clutched a backpack with her papers and some clothes, as she endured the last and most important leg of her journey.

Darnya turned around to say something, and she stopped. Lindy was shaking.

"Lindy, are you okay?" asked Darnya. Maksym glanced in his rearview mirror. The lord didn't look good.

"No, I'm not." Lindy paused, "But don't worry; when we get to the checkpoint, I'll settle down. I always do. Right now, I don't know what to expect. It's nerve-wracking."

"We'll be fine. This is going to go as smooth as butter. The EN intel people have been gaming every possibility for days now." Darnya tried to be soothing, but Lindy just shook her head.

"*You'll* be fine. *Maksym* will be fine. I can see that. But I don't know if *I'll* be fine. I can only hope my future is so intertwined with yours that I'll have the same result."

"Well, no one knows the fut –"

"I do. Why do you think my name is The Fortuneteller?" she snapped. "I can read any human's future, but I can't read a lord's, and that includes my own. You guys, you humans, are an open book."

Darnya stared at Lindy. No, it had never occurred to her that *Fortuneteller* was anything other than a stage name. The lord had never hidden her talent after all; it had been right there every time they used her name.

"Oh. I didn't know that you could really read the future. I thought *Fortuneteller* was just a part of your Gypsy thing. A cover."

Lindy was testy. "Why would you think that? I'm a witch. Once you came clean with me, I came clean with you. I haven't hidden who I am, not to you two."

Darnya was embarrassed. "We know a lot of lords, Lindy. And they all do things like fly or zap things with their powers or make wind blow or bend light – that sort of thing. I've never met a lord who could tell the future. It never occurred to me. Maksym and I were wondering what you *did*, not what you could *see*."

"Oh." Lindy considered this. "Why didn't you just ask?"

"Because in lord-world it's rude to ask a lord about their abilities. It's like asking what their sex lives are like. It's personal."

"I think," Maksym added, "that it's also a matter of being careful who you're talking to. If people know a lord's limits, you lose an advantage, and the world is still dangerous even to the most powerful lords. If you say you can kill a hundred men with a look, then a bad guy will send a hundred and one men after you."

Lindy nodded, very true. "Well, then, I won't tell you what I can physically do. I'll keep that nugget to myself. But my big witchery is reading the future. I've scanned you, Darnya, and every human I've met in the last day. I'll be scanning the guys at the border post. I can't change their futures easily, and I won't have time to do that. But if I walk up to the passport guy and I see that his future is disappearing and he's going to be dead in a few minutes, I'll know something bad is going to happen. That's something I can do. And by knowing that sometimes I can change the future."

"Sometimes?" said Darnya.

"Sometimes."

Maksym was intrigued. "How can you change the future?"

"Anyone can change the future. You have free will, and every choice, everything you do, changes the future. If I know a person is going to zig, then I zag. I change the future by altering what I'm going to do, usually by avoiding confrontation, but not always. When I tore that orc's artery, I changed his future, that's for sure. And I changed mine. I wouldn't have called you for help if he hadn't died, and I probably wouldn't be sitting in the back of this car now."

"Can you tell me my future?"

Lindy looked at Darnya and smiled. "Sure, but do you really want to know? If I told you that you were going to have a baby next year and it was going to be a great scientist, that is a future I see today. But with knowledge, you can use your free will to change it. What if you didn't want a baby and had an abortion? You've just made a different future. And that scientist would never be, and that could change the future of millions – maybe everyone."

Lindy looked out the window. "I told you that you would live to see Canada. Telling you that is a risk for me because I don't know if I will. Maybe you'll get careless because you know you won't die. Maybe you'll change how you do things, and that will hurt me. I don't think so, but who knows? I don't *know* because I can't read my own future. If I could do that, I'd be paralysed with possibilities, so all I can do is what you humans do. Study the facts and play the odds. Hope I make good decisions."

Maksym glanced back. "We'll find out soon. We're almost there. First phase is starting."

And with that, a pick-up moved in front of their car and flashed its brakes. An electrician's van pulled behind them and blinked its headlights. They were soon surrounded by a knot of traffic, all of whom were RumLot Security operatives.

They drove under a green highway sign. *Canada 4 miles.*

Then another sign. *ALL Cars Leaving the US Must STOP for Inspection.*

That was a new procedure instituted under Meechum to prevent lords from leaving the US and making Canada and Europe stronger. Before, a traveller only had to prove their citizenship when entering Canada and Mexico. Now he had to prove his tribe when he left, and that meant a border stop on both sides.

It was also a nice little money maker for the US Treasury – 20USD from every passenger as a departure fee.

There were more signs. Signs that said *EXIT ONLY to MAIN ST.* Signs that pointed to lanes for semis and signs directing to lanes reserved for passenger cars and small trucks.

And signs saying that *Harbouring NON-HUMANS is a FEDERAL CRIME, Punishable with a $10,000 fine and two years imprisonment.*

The car slowed. The pick-up in front stopped, and a Border Patrol officer walked up to it with a scanner in his hand and scanned the driver's passport, looked at it, looked at the driver, then handed it back and waved him on.

Then Maksym stopped, and a uniformed woman walked up to the driver's side and looked in.

"Hi! Could I please have your passports?"

Darnya and Maksym handed their passports over, and Lindy passed up her documents. The officer made a face when she received the Form 4029. She scanned Maksym's and Darnya's passports and handed them back.

Then she looked at the Form 4029 and leaned into the window and spoke directly to Lindy.

"Ma'am, I need you to get out of the car. I have to verify that you are human."

Maksym started to protest, but she cut him off. "Look, I know it's inconvenient, but it will only take a minute. No fuss, and you go on your way. But it has to be done."

"Maksym, I'm okay." And before he could say anything, Lindy was out of the car.

"I'm sorry, Ma'am, but I'm going to have to look at your eyes."

Lindy nodded; the woman looked and saw brown eyes and marked that on her device.

"Ma'am, can you please take off the bonnet?"

Darnya leaned forward, her hand under the jacket lying across her lap, holding her pistol. Maksym pressed his door latch, releasing it.

Gen Jameson, the RumLot Security professionals, Canadian police, reps from the Canadian Department of Elf Affairs, and about twenty elves waited with the horses and the caravan in a secure warehouse. They watched what was going on from a video feed from the car's dash cam.

Everyone held their breath.

Lindy was appalled. "In front of all of these men? Do you want to do a roadside strip search, too?"

The woman had the grace to look embarrassed. "I'm sorry, ma'am, but those are the regs. I have to check to see if you're an elf or something. These forms don't guarantee you're a human; they're too old. Next month, the new forms will have a line on them telling us you've been checked out and aren't un-human. Until then, we have to check you."

"This isn't right. You know it's not right." But she untied the bonnet strings and lifted it up, and then just as fast as it went up, she jammed it back down again. She only had a glimpse, but the officer saw that the Amish woman had light brown hair and no elf ears and marked that on the device.

“Thank you for cooperating. Here’s your paperwork, and I hope you have a nice trip to Canada.”

Lindy didn’t say anything, just looked huffy and flounced back to the car and slammed the door.

Maksym quietly locked the car door again and drove off. No one said a word.

It took three minutes to get to the Canadian side and another two minutes to get through passport control.

It was a pity that Lindy couldn’t hear the cheers in the warehouse.

That was probably because she, Darnya, and Maksym were all screaming for joy.

There was another fifteen-minute ride to the warehouse, and that’s when Darnya asked Lindy how she had hidden her ears; the lord just rolled her eyes.

“A wig, of course, with fake wax ears in the hair, and it’s damned uncomfortable, too. I’ve done this sort of thing before. This isn’t the first time someone has come up to make sure I’m not a witch. I’ve worn wigs for hundreds of years. The contacts are a new thing. I’ll be happy to get rid of both. I hate the contacts; they hurt.”

Maksym grinned in the rearview mirror. “Then take’m all off! You can now! You’re almost home!”

So she did.

Lord Aethelind

Events went very, very fast.

Lindy was reunited with her horses and her caravan and met the entire team that was working on her case. She couldn't believe the number of people who were involved, and while most were only on the Lord Aethelind Project for a few days (for security reasons), some, like Gen Jameson, were watching and pulling strings from the first day she was identified.

She met her first elves, an emotional meeting she would never forget. When she met her first elf, the solitary witch faded into the past, and Lord Aethelind moved to the present. Her life alone ended because now she would always have her clan elves and lords. All she had to do was stand in the bare, echoing warehouse and shake the hand of an elf and look in his eyes, and she was clan-bonded.

When Gen Jameson asked her what her next steps were, and she hesitated, he jumped in with the suggestion that she go to Aelfeham House and learn about being a lord before she made any decisions.

"Take some time to adjust to your new world. It's a big change! The horses and the caravan can go with you, no problem at all. You can leave and come back any time, no cost to you."

He looked at her kindly. "I know you've been around a long time, but there's always more to learn. Give yourself time to learn and adjust. You have forever."

She looked around the empty warehouse. There was a big spread set up on folding tables at one end; the RumLot employees were going to have an "End-of-Project" party and celebrate another winning mission. She saw Darnya and Maksym talking and laughing with some guys, and she was sure they were operatives (wasn't Darnya something they call a Ranger?), like they were. Everyone was giddy with the successful Lord extraction, and Lindy heard music coming from a speaker. Someone sprayed a bottle of champagne on Maksym, starting more cheers.

It was an End-of-Project winding-up party for the RumLot people, but Lindy knew her Lord Aethelind Project was just beginning.

"That sounds sensible, Gen Jameson. But could I have a minute alone to thank Darnya and Maksym first? If the elves want to get the horses ready to go, that's fine; I'll only be a minute."

Darnya and Maksym were called over, and Lindy thanked them, tears welling up in her bright green eyes.

"Darnya, you asked me to tell you your future. All I'm going to say is that from what I see at this point, it's going to be a happy one. I won't get into specifics –" and she bent down to whisper in Darnya's ear, " – because I don't want you to fuck it up."

Then she turned to Maksym, who was still wiping champagne from his eyes.

"I need to talk to you privately." And she grabbed his arm and pulled him far enough away that Darnya and Gen Jameson couldn't hear her. She made him bend down so she could whisper in his ear.

"In eighteen months, Darnya is going to be married to the love of her life. In two years, she'll be a mother. If you fuck this up, it won't be with you, and the baby won't be yours. Or maybe it will. Don't forget what I said about free will. Futures can be changed."

She looked back at Darnya and Jameson, and they weren't alone. A man had walked up and was talking to Darnya. One of the operatives. He was smiling down at her and was handing her a beer.

Maksym looked at Darnya, then looked at the Fortuneteller, who raised an eyebrow.

"It was an honour, Lindy. Really nice meeting you. Give me a call sometime. I think –" And he was gone.

A half hour later, Lindy was standing under a circus tent in the middle of a green Suffolk lawn and being welcomed to Aelfeham House by Lord Jack and Lord Alizah.

Lindy

Every afternoon, Lindy had an hour in the Lesson Room with Gerald and did everything he asked of her. If he asked her to move a plate, she was happy to do it, and the porcelain flew around the room like flying saucers on crack. She could juggle them. She could, just like Lord Freyja, serve herself on a buffet while holding the plate aloft and throwing food on it. She could lift up to five hundred pounds of dead weight at a time. She could lob rocks and projectiles like a cannon.

She could tear things, which was of profound interest to Victor, and he and Gerald spent two days watching her tear paper, rags, and then, in one grisly experiment, a couple of live chickens. It was, she said, just like when she did any levitation magic, doing two things at once. She just levitated one side of something to the left and the other side to the right, and the thing she was pulling in two different directions tore in two. Easy.

She told Victor during the chicken experiment that she didn't have to tear an attacker into huge chunks; just a tiny part of his interior body was enough. A rip in the brain, a torn main artery, they were much more efficient and much less tiring to her. And if she was careful, totally untraceable to her. When she said that, Gerald thought Victor was going to bond to her or something; he looked like he was in love. Lord Aethelind was the perfect assassin.

If Gerald asked her to disappear, something she couldn't do it. She couldn't do anything that had to do with waves or particles, or gravity. She couldn't manipulate water or air, create fire, or heat or cool things.

She couldn't port herself like Lord Sarah, a previously unknown ability. Nor could she read minds like Lord Judy, another previously unknown ability. Gerald really thought she could do that. But no.

The elf knew she was an Elemental; every elf and most lords could feel it. Her eyes glowed bright green with power, but all he could see her do was lift stuff, which any middling lord could do. Yes, she was really good at it, but five hundred pounds worth of lift strength was not an Elemental ability.

Lord Aethelind said she could read the futures of humans and orcs. She couldn't read the future of an elf or a lord. She told Gerald she could predict outcomes, possibilities, paths, and, depending on how interested she was, she could read clear to the end of a human's short life. She had no idea if she could read more than one hundred years into the future because humans didn't usually make it further than that.

Gerald didn't want to say that reading the future was impossible because no one could manipulate time, but it was. He sighed. This lord thought she was reading the future, which no one could really do because the future hadn't happened yet, so what was she really doing?

So Gerald worked with her whenever he had a new idea, and in the meantime, Lord Aethelind worked on her moving things ability with cheerful goodwill and practised constantly. At least she set a good example for the young ones.

For her part, Lindy wasn't worried about what Gerald thought. She knew what she could do and not do, and the moving things practise made her feel better and kept her young. The freedom to move things in public whenever she wanted was great! After living in the shadows for over four hundred years, the ability to throw a plate across the back lawn of Aelfeham House as hard as she wanted and not give a shit who saw was liberating.

Just not having to wear a turban or a wig made her want to shake her hair out and twirl. It was intoxicating to finally be what she was born to be – a lord.

So when Gerald said that she must be doing something else and not reading the future, maybe massive probability calculations, she just shrugged and smiled and went on with her long life.

She wasn't very good during Victor's PE lessons. She was a slow runner, not interested in combat, and, like Lord Judy, pretty clumsy. Not as spatially inept as Lord Judy, but close. Victor thought she was going to lose a finger the first time she tried throwing an elf knife.

That meant, to Victor's disappointment, that she simply wasn't suitable for Ranger or Warrior Lord training. He signed her off as fully capable of self-defence because she could kill anyone just by looking at them, and there's nothing more self-defending than that.

In his report to Lord James, he said, "Lord Aethelind is not suitable for solo work as a Ranger or Warrior Lord where a wide range of offensive skills would be needed, but in some special circumstances she could be very useful as part of a team. She is quite comfortable with outdoor activities like camping, hiking, mountain climbing, and riding, so she is not limited to urban work. She is a competent shot with a pistol or a rifle, but not more than competent (see her range scores, attached)."

So, as the threats from outside the EN bubble heated up, Lindy was assigned as an emergency guard to the children's wing if Aelfeham House was ever attacked. It was one of those duties that no one ever expected to do, but in the event of a dire emergency, she knew her post. She was fine with that; it gave her a job to do.

She was offered a real job to port to the EN embassy in Poland four days a week and act as a liaison and "visible lord" for visitors. Like Adem, she was to lead tours, schmooze with visiting diplomats and Polish officials, and generally look good and give visitors a chance to say "I shook hands with a lord. She was lovely." Why Poland? Because she said she might have been born in Poland. No other reason.

Lindy was very happy to do it. All her life, she'd worked at making her clients happy, and talking with humans was easy. Now that she was dressed in an EN red uniform and didn't have to wear a turban or wig, it was doubly easy. Using Adem's transport nodes, she would leave Aelfeham House in the morning and come back at four, and the more she did it and became comfortable with her duties, the more she liked it. She was told she'd have a four-week trial period, and if she liked the job and the head Counsel of the Embassy liked her (a human woman she hadn't met yet), she would be offered a permanent position. Alizah told her not to worry about the Counsel. They had been lobbying for a lord to work there for years. They were thrilled when they found out she was coming.

In the meantime, she started training with Adem at the London Embassy.

Integrating socially with the lords of Aelfeham House was much more slow-going. Over the years, Lindy found Romani clans to join, and she wasn't overwhelmed by Aelfeham House's communal dinners or put off by the cliques, but she was shy in this new world. She kept to herself at first, not sure if she would be welcome if she invited herself to the group activities.

In her old world, she had been in a group, but still not *in* the group. Individual Roma she'd lived with might have grown to like her over time, but after you see an attacker fall down dead because your "auntie" threw a hex at him, it's hard to have a really close relationship. What if she got mad at you? You don't become good friends with someone you're afraid of. So in four hundred years, she'd never had a lover other than her one-night stand with David (the number of lords she was teaching who had *no* sex life was something sex-ed teacher Sylvia could never get over) or a girlfriend to share confidences with about the said lover. In her last fifty years, she'd had no clan at all; the "niece" she had moved to Chicago with had passed on, and no one replaced her.

But the other lords were kind and welcoming, especially after the dressing down they'd gotten from the Primary over Lord Freyja. Lindy's diffidence was recognised for what it was – a bit of social awkwardness and not snobbery or hostility – and people tried a little harder. She tried harder as well, and gradually everyone became a little more comfortable around each other.

Maria

Maria walked into Girl's Movie Night with an expression on her face that was so self-satisfied that everyone had to laugh at her. When Rita asked why she was just grinning to herself for no apparent reason, Maria blurted it out. It wasn't as if she could hold it in one single second more.

"I have a date with Lord Ayu!" And she curtsied to one and all.

OOoooooh. The ladies were impressed. Ever since Lord Ayu showed up, he had been the subject of intense speculation by one and all of the fair sex, bonded and not. The bonded ones thought watching the single women chasing after the full-moon lord was good sport, and they teased their sisters unmercifully, especially since he didn't seem much interested in any of them.

But now Maria had a date! How had she managed that?

Maria plopped on the couch, squeezed in between Lindy and Talia, and immediately began to hog the popcorn.

"I saw him on the terrace, just sitting there, and no one else was around –"

"So you jumped him." Maria shot Rita a dirty look, but she was smiling. Winners can afford to be gracious.

"I didn't *jump* him. I walked up and said hi, nice night. I wanted to talk to him about something – *anything!* – and I mentioned that back in South America we had terraces like this, but they were full of orchids, not geraniums and pansies, and that got him talking about flowers, and we talked about that for a few minutes, and I said I liked orchids the best, but England doesn't have any, and he said that wasn't true, and he offered to show me some."

She sat back and grinned at the TV. "So tomorrow we're going on a hike, and he's going to show me some native orchids."

Maria turned to Talia. "And *that* qualifies as a date!"

Everyone agreed that Maria's hike with Lord Ayu certainly qualified as a date. The guy had asked her out, they'd set a time, and they were going somewhere, just the two of them. A date by any definition.

Lindy smiled at Maria's glee. She was the first one they knew of (and the GSN would know for sure) that Lord Ayu had asked out. But Lindy knew, even though she had no experience with dates and romance and all that, that the odds of anything like a bonding coming out of it were tiny. Maria was very pretty, but she was also very young, only just twenty, and while Ayu was physically a very, very attractive thirty-five-ish, mentally, he was of vast age. They had nothing in common to build a relationship on, not that Lindy could see. British wild orchids would not be enough.

But, hey, they could have a few hours of really hot sex, and that might be enough for both of them.

The women watched the rom-com, laughed at the humans and their quirks (the heroine was ageing out of fertility and needed a man to make a baby with, but didn't want to marry, blah, blah), and teased Maria about her hot date with the flaming hot Lord Ayu.

Lindy

There must have been something in the air because the next day, right out of the blue, Lindy was asked out on a date, too.

She rushed into the Breakfast Room, intent on getting a good breakfast in before she ported to the London Embassy, where she was still training with Adem, when Paulo sat down opposite her and asked what her plans were for the day.

In mid-bite of her doughnut, Lindy looked at him, wondering why he wanted to know, but he just smiled and cocked his head. Was she going to answer?

"I have to meet Adem, and we're going to take a bunch of junior officers from the Royal Navy around the Embassy and talk about our mission and how it relates to theirs."

"Well, that won't take all day. When are you going to break for lunch? If you want some company, I'll meet you."

Lindy sat back, gobsmacked. The man was setting up a lunch date. Just like that. She was so discombobulated that she said, "Twelve."

And he grinned and got up. "I'll see you at twelve then, in the public cafe. I think the food's better there. See you then!" And he left before she could say anything else.

Rita sat down with her plate in his chair and cut into her fried eggs.

"You look like you've just been hit. Sugar rush?"

Lindy looked at her. “Paulo just asked me out to lunch. I didn’t say no. I didn’t know what to say.”

“I was right, then. Sugar rush.” And she grinned. “He has the hots for you, y’know.”

“No!”

“Yes! Anyone can see it. He’s been watching you since you walked in the door.”

“No!”

Rita rolled her eyes. How could this woman not notice Paulo? He was cute! Yes, he was only thirty-one, and his eyes were a medium blue, so he wasn’t Elemental material, but he was clever, ambitious, and was doing interesting things with RumLot Security. He wasn’t a Gary (who had now become the single ladies' shorthand for Primary Loser), not by any means. Rita wouldn’t mind going out with Paulo herself.

So she said so. “If you have lunch and he’s not for you, just steer him my way. I think he’s cute.”

“Sure – but I’m still adjusting to the fact that he asked me out at all. I never thought of him that way.”

“Do you think of any guy *that* way? You have trouble asking a man to pass the salt.”

Lindy looked down at her own plate, now untouched, and Rita was immediately sorry she’d made that crack. “Look, Lindy, it’s just lunch. He’s asking for you to give him a little one-on-one time, and if you find out that he’s not worth a second hour, you don’t accept any invites again. It’s a toe-dip in the pond to test the water, not a full-fledged dive.”

She sighed. "You're right; I'm just startled, that's all. Men don't like me, and when someone does, it throws me off."

Rita raised an eyebrow. "Well, if guys see you out with Paulo, expect a rush of'm. When one guy is seen as successful, they all think they have a chance. *Human* men might not like you, but to the single lord guys, you're a hot tamale. They think your ears are sexy – didn't Sylvia talk to you about that? They think you're beautiful, *and* you're an Elemental. Humans are money snobs, and lords are ability snobs, and Lindy, you have ability. Anyone can see that."

Blinking back a tear, Lindy smiled gratefully at Rita. "Thanks, Rita, that's really sweet of you."

Rita rolled her eyes. "Shit, it's the truth. Now you go and fix your makeup and head to work. I want to know what happens. I have no life of my own, so let me live vicariously."

After Lindy left, Rita shook her head and smiled to herself. Ah, well, if Lindy fell for Paulo, that left Dennis and Joey. Single lords were thin on the ground, but she wasn't reduced to Zhan. Not yet. Hell, she'd wait fifty years for one of the baby boys to grow up before she was desperate enough to bed Zhan.

Adem and Lindy

Adem was waiting for her, as he always did, and as usual was as sweet as pie. Lindy loved Adem; she loved his enthusiasm and admired his cleverness. She could see why so many of their guests thought he was a bit lightweight, but that was just a persona he cultivated. His bubbly good humour and high-energy enthusiasm for the most mundane tour was a bit over the top at times, but she saw on their first day out that he was a master manipulator of humans. He made them all think they were special, and when the tour was over, he'd have all sorts of information that he had gleaned from the most taciturn, grumpy visitor.

He enjoyed it. Getting people to love and support the EN was part of his mission, but many of the tours brought in delegations and mid-level bureaucrats from friendly countries from all over the world, the people who really knew what was going on in their departments, and the nuggets of information gleaned from chatty sub-assistant directors of whatever were all useful to the intel people in the back rooms.

Lindy was learning, and Adem was a master teacher. Her years sitting across from giggling girls, worried matrons, and desperate men and pretending to divine their fortunes in her Tarot cards, gave her good training for reading body language. And, of course, she really could read their futures.

In contrast to the effervescent Adem, the men in the tours thought Lindy was exotic and beautiful, something that never ceased to amaze her. She guessed it was all a matter of environment. When her old clients walked into her dark caravan and saw the mysterious Fortuneteller in her heavy make-up and turban, weirdly lit by a single candle, they were frightened. Lord Aethelind, on the other hand, had light-touch modern make-up, huge elf ears, and a thick white braid that fell down to her waist. Who could be frightened of her little heart-shaped, dimpled face with the huge, glowing green eyes? She was hot. Same woman, different setting.

This morning's tour was mostly young(ish) men and women in their last year of speciality officer training in the UK Military. They were from all branches, but their common goal was to work as liaisons with the EN. For many of them, this wasn't their first tour of the EN Embassy. For some, it wasn't even their second. So Adem wanted to mix it up for them and do something a bit different to keep them engaged with the EN and feed into their sense of wonder. He also wanted to send a message. Caddy and Conary wanted to amp up the public perception of the lords' powers. They felt some humans were getting a bit bored with lords, a bit complacent.

Because he knew of Lindy's ability to move things, he asked her to set up a little magic show and juggle some plates or something and show what she could do. Adem was well aware that watching his own very powerful ability was about as exciting as watching grass grow. Creating bubbles outside of space and time was awesome to the lords who understood it, but it wasn't good theatre.

When the tour was over, it ended in the big ballroom on the top floor. Adem bounced into the centre of the huge space and waved all the officers, about twenty of them, to come to him.

"Now I know that most of you have been here before, so I'm going to give you a special treat so you don't get bored with us." With a flourish, he beckoned Lindy in, and she smiled. A year ago, she would never have dreamt that she would be demonstrating her magic, ears exposed and eyes glowing, *in public* to a bunch of military officers.

"This is my gorgeous colleague, Lord Aethelind. She's agreed to give you a little demonstration of a lord's abilities. You know we usually don't do this, mostly for security reasons, but you are a special group, and I think you'll find it educational."

A young woman, looking at Lindy's red uniform, raised her hand. "Is Lord Aethelind an Elemental like you, Lord Adem?"

Adem grinned. "We don't talk about individual abilities; it's rather rude. It's like talking about your bank account or sex life. A bit private. You judge for yourself. Personally, I don't have any idea what she is going to do. I asked her to put on a little show, and she said yes."

Lindy walked to the centre and bowed to Adem. "Thank you, Lord Adem, for the lovely introduction." She cocked her head and looked at the group. "I thought a plate show would be interesting."

Most of them had seen a plate show before, which was a lord lifting and floating a plate around the room. They smiled, but the lack of enthusiasm was palpable. Most just wanted to get to lunch.

Lindy's eyes barely glowed, but a dozen plates flew off a credenza and floated into the circle and in front of the officers. They hovered in place, unmoving.

"Now, if the nearest person can please pass the plate to your colleague."

But no one could move them, not an inch. They leaned on them, but nothing moved. Some of the bigger guys were bodybuilders, and they really tried to put some force into it. They couldn't move the plates.

Adem grinned, delighted. "Notice that she's holding up twelve of them at once! How much power do you think it takes to keep them floating in mid-air, against gravity and against your muscles!"

The officers started chattering amongst themselves, and little groups gathered around the plates, pushing and pulling and trying to get them to move, when all the plates started to rise. One guy grabbed a plate and wouldn't let go, and soon he was hanging from it, his feet not touching the ground.

“How high, sir, do you want to go? This ballroom ceiling must be about thirty feet high.”

He gripped hard, his knuckles white. “Ma’am, I don’t want to break anything if I fall.”

“You won’t fall.” She moved two of the plates under his feet so that he was standing on them, and they lifted him to the ceiling and brought him down again. Then, when he was back on the ground, she magically gathered up all the plates into a single pile and flew them back to the credenza to the applause of the officers.

Lindy hadn't broken a sweat, but her eyes were glowing. Adem smiled and ended the tour.

“And that, ladies and gentlemen, is a very short demonstration of what a lord can do. Lord Aethlind, thank you. Goodbye to all, and thank you for coming.”

Adem knew that the entire plate show would be dissected in intelligence offices worldwide. One lord could levitate twelve objects at once. They would calculate the amount of force the officers had pushed against the places and how much energy that had taken. They would examine her range. They would make the classic mistake of assuming a cute female lord of average height must be weaker than a large male lord, so if she could do that, what could a man do? And they would note that this was someone they had never seen before, a total unknown. How many other unknown lords did the EN have hidden? Was she an Elemental? She was in a red uniform.

It was a demonstration of raw power, and sometimes a demonstration was enough to prevent stupid actions.

They would do more demos as the EN's enemies became bolder and more aggressive.

Paulo and Lindy

Lunch with Paulo was fun. He was waiting with a table when she walked into the public restaurant, very handsome in the navy uniform of a working lord. He stood up as she walked up to the table, and for a second, she wondered if he was going to tell her he had to leave, but no, he pulled her chair out for her, an old-fashioned courtesy that had never been offered to Lindy before. She didn't know quite what to do. So she sat down.

He was charming, chatted about the crowded restaurant, made sure she ordered a good lunch, and after a few minutes, Lindy relaxed and they talked, and by the end of the lunch, they were laughing. After exactly an hour, she left for her next tour with Adem, and he left to port back to RumLot HQ, where he was working as a drone pilot patrolling the Wall and gathering intelligence as the Russians manoeuvred on their own side of the barrier. It was a good job, he said, and a flexible jumping off point to other careers once his abilities kicked in and he knew what he could do.

He told some very funny stories about what he had seen as a drone pilot, and he told her a little bit about his past life in Colombia, where he'd lived in a small town and worked in his parents' business. His family had sheltered him from outsiders, and he'd been happy while he was growing up, just a normal oddball, really. But when his glowing eyes and news about what lords could do garnered attention from the local drug mafia, he had to escape. He didn't talk about his traumatic journey north or his time in the Texas prison. That was for later. All he said to Lindy was that his life now was almost perfect, and joining the EN was the best thing he'd ever done.

He never asked about her abilities or her future goals or her past, but she didn't notice that omission. Later that night, Lindy met Rita in the TV room, where Lindy gave Rita a line-by-line report of the lunch, and Rita noticed Paulo's lack of curiosity right away. Asked if she would go out again with him, Lindy frowned and considered it. Probably.

To Rita, Paulo's lack of curiosity and Lindy's hesitation spoke volumes. She sipped her wine and turned to watch the game show on TV. Lindy was flattered by the attention but not enamoured. Paulo was setting out his stall, wooing the lord, but not wooing the woman. He wanted a wife to make his almost-perfect life perfect. Lindy was a good catch in a very small pool of fish, and Paulo was smart enough to see it. He was also smart enough to see that her aloofness with the single men at Aelfeham House wasn't because she was a snobby Elemental lord but because she was shy.

Rita smiled. Maybe Paulo would be back on her list of prospects sooner than she'd thought. He hadn't captured Lindy's heart – not yet, probably not ever – but you never know. She wondered what it would take for Paulo to really fall in love. That was an interesting question.

Lindy and Adem

When Lindy wasn't at the embassy in London, she was messing with her horses or taking Lord Classes. The four days a week that she was in London, she worked under Adem, learning the trade of public relations, intelligence gathering, basic schmoozing, and advanced buttering-up. They generally took two tour groups out in the morning, had lunch, then two short ones in the afternoon, unless there was some really important bigwig to see; then they would take up the entire afternoon. On Fridays, Adem ported to wherever the week's elves were raised and created a transport node there. Each node took him about ten minutes to make, as long as a local worthy didn't hold him up.

Lunch was fun. She'd sit with either Adem, Malachi, Trevor, Germain, Judy, or Vrt, depending on who was around. It was an ever-changing table because "stuff" came up all the time, and people were busy. Malachi was there the least because he had duties with Mordecai, raising elves.

The day after her date with Paulo, Lindy found herself in the employee restaurant having lunch with Trevor, Germaine, Malachi, and Adem.

Maybe it was because of her recent lunch with Paulo or even her fling with David, but she seemed a bit more sensitive to the politics of romance lately. Germaine and Trevor lived together and bickered and fussed over each other like an old married couple. They were obviously mad about each other.

She read their futures – nice and long and happy, both of them. There was even an adopted child in about five years, but she didn't tell them that. Telling them might change things if they tried too hard or too early. Best to let that thread develop naturally.

Malachi and Adem, now that was a puzzle. She wished she could read their futures, but she couldn't. When Adem wasn't looking, Malachi would watch him. When Malachi was talking with someone else, Adem's eyes would be glued to the Warrior Lord. They never touched each other, not like lovers would, and certainly not the way Trevor and Germaine did. Germaine couldn't keep his hands off Trevor, always picking lint from his suit or adjusting his pocket square.

Adem's and Malachi's smells weren't quite right, and Lindy didn't know enough about bonding to understand what was going on.

Malachi, Trevor, and Germaine left to go to their afternoon appointments, and Lindy and Adem stayed back, enjoying a long lunch. They had an hour before they had to leave for their next tour.

As Malachi left, Adem watched him walk out, and the longing in his eyes – it made Lindy sad just to see him.

"Why don't you ask him out?"

Adem started, like she had pricked him with a pin. "Who?"

"You know who. Malachi. Why don't you ask him out?" She looked at the lord and smiled. "He likes you. You like him. You're attracted to each other. I don't think either of you has some other lover in your pockets. Why not?"

Adem turned bright red. "You don't understand. We have history. He didn't like me and said so."

"It seems like he likes you a lot now. He's a quiet one, Malachi, but intense. Very intense. Sometimes, intense people get a bit emphatic. They speak before they think." She sipped her coffee. "Y'know, Adem, you're old. I'm old. I've never had anyone fall in love with me. It's a rare, rare thing; you're lucky if that happens to you. If someone ever falls in love with me and I love him, I wouldn't risk losing him because he once said something stupid. We all say stupid things, make mistakes. Was Malachi's stupidity a deal breaker? A reason to be alone forever?"

Adem cupped his tea in his shaking hands and shook his head no.

"If he didn't love you then, then he certainly loves you now." Her voice softened, and Adem looked at the lord. Her eyes glowed bright. "My ability is time, Adem. No one believes me, but it's true. I read it, study it, and test it. I can't read your future, but I know some things. Future time is just a probability, a suggestion. Free will can change the future. All of our futures are intertwined, so reading them can get very complicated, but anyone can see that Malachi and you are heading to one future now, apart. But a move by either of you will change that. Time is water, it isn't stone. It flows. You can change the flow."

The Fortuneteller smiled, leaned forward, and patted her friend's hand. "Ask him."

Adem and Malachi

Malachi was back in his flat after archery practice and just taking off his boots when he heard a knock at his door.

It was Adem. He looked really upset, and seeing Adem upset made Malachi scowl, which had the effect of making Adem more upset.

"Hey, what's up? Is something wrong?"

Adem cleared his throat and shifted. Malachi had never seen the man look so uncomfortable. This must be bad.

"Well, spit it out, man. Whatever it is, we'll deal with it."

"I was wondering –" He coughed again. "If you'd like to go out with me. Like on a date. Dinner or something –"

Oh. Shit. Malachi just stared. Adem stared back. Then it was Malachi's turn to stumble and stutter. He turned and walked back into his living room, and Adem followed him, shutting the door. When he heard the door click shut, Malachi spun back around.

"Adem, I'd like to go to dinner with you. I'd love to date you – but I can't."

Adem stopped, and his face scrunched. Here it was again. He wasn't up to Malachi's standard. He straightened up. They might as well get this over with now.

"Why not?"

"Because I love you."

Well. That was unexpected. Malachi looked at Adem, and the look of puzzlement and hurt on his face was unbearable. He tried to explain.

"Adem – we're going to war soon. Very soon. I'm a Warrior Lord. Defending elves and lords, it's what I do." He took a deep breath.

"I'm bonded to you, and if you die, I'll die too. I'm okay with that. You die, and I have a pistol and plenty of ammo, and I know what to do. But it probably won't happen. You're going to be in the rear, and you're powerful, but if the worst happens, you'll just go to ground and turn into a mushroom again. I *want* you to turn into a mushroom again!

"But if we start dating, I won't be able to keep my hands off of you. If you bond with me, then you're at risk because I'm at risk. I'm not going to be in the rear; I'm the tip of the spear. I can't – I won't – let you die because of what I am. I won't. You're too important, too precious to lose because you're bonded to a soldier. The EN can lose a Warrior Lord, but it can't lose an Adem."

Adem just stood there, tears running down his face. "I love you, Kai."

"I love you, too, Adem." He sighed. "Now get the fuck out of here. I stink."

Adem turned and walked to the door, and it was all Malachi could do not to run up and grab him and put all of his good intentions in the garbage pile.

He stopped, his hand on the doorknob. "Kai, after this war, can we go out for coffee?"

Malachi made a sound somewhere between a chuckle and a sob. "Yeah, it's a date. I know a good place. I'll even treat you."

Adem nodded and left, shutting the door softly behind him.

Lindy

Lindy didn't see Paulo for a couple of days, then he showed up for lunch again at the embassy. He'd watched her schedule in the master scheduler on their EN phone apps and knew when she was free at the same time he was and texted her. Lunch again? She said yes.

And that's the way it went for a couple of weeks while she finished up training under Adem. In the meantime, Rita was right, as she usually was when it came to the complicated mating rituals of the lords. When it got out that Lindy was having lunch with Paulo, other lords began to get interested in her. What one man desired, the others wanted, too, and suddenly she had Joey, Anime, and Zhan making a point of sitting next to her at dinner and in the evenings when the single lords left their bedrooms to relax in the common areas.

It was a bit overwhelming. Actually, it was a lot overwhelming. Zahn was aggressive. Not to Lindy, never to Lindy, but to the other male lords. He wasn't afraid of a little dominance posturing in front of the other men, and there were a couple of times when they got testy with each other, and Rita had to step in.

Lindy had no idea how to handle them. She wasn't a flirt, and she didn't find their sniping at each other amusing, not at all. She felt, as she said to Talia privately, not like a prize but like prey. Their attention wasn't flattering after the first few minutes because, in the end, it wasn't about *her*; it was about what they wanted to do with her. And since she wasn't horny for them, it was all off-putting. Annoying.

Talia just laughed, remembering when she went from bottom level, just-Chi's-girlfriend, to desirable prospect and how Jan was shut out by the scrum.

"These guys all have raging lord hormones, and most of them haven't had any chance of a girl paying attention to them sometimes for decades. All of a sudden, they're not the freaks who have to hide but are mixed in with some very sexy women. They're like kangaroo bucks who've moved from the isolated bachelor herds and are now mixed in with the does. They don't quite know what to do, so they operate on instinct. And instinct says if the doe wants a beer, they'll get her a beer, and if another buck sits next to her when they're away at the bar, they get mad."

Lindy rolled her eyes. "I feel like I need to watch more Attenborough. Y'know, when I watch the nature docs and see the stags fighting, the does are all in the background, eating grass and ignoring them. Maybe that's what I should do. Go eat some grass."

Talia chuckled and nodded.

Three days later, that's exactly what Lindy did. Zahn was regaling Lindy with his prowess as a fighter back when he was a nomad in Mongolia, and Joey rolled his eyes and pointed out that Victor was always looking for Warrior Lord prospects, and why didn't Zahn go volunteer for that? Zahn got mad, Joey sniped back, and Lindy suddenly stood up and announced to the table she was going to go eat some grass, which made Talia and Rita choke. Jan just looked puzzled at his bond-wife and hit her on the back.

"Are you okay?"

Talia just nodded, her eyes wet with tears, and she coughed again.

So while everyone was paying attention to Talia's coughing fit, Lindy disappeared.

She ended up on the terrace. There was no fire, and a housekeeper elf popped up and asked her if she wanted it lit, and she shook her head no. She didn't want to draw attention to herself. Then do you want a beer or anything? A hamburger? No, but she changed her mind and asked for a bottle of cider. A minute later, he came back with a blanket and a hot cider, which was lovely.

It was equally lovely sitting on the terrace. A few stars winked between the clouds, and for the first time in weeks, Lindy was alone in the quiet, snuggled against the cold in a heavy blanket, and sipping the hot cider.

There was a clatter. An "Oh, shit!" And then "Sorry – I knocked over my bottle."

She wasn't alone after all. On the other side of the terrace was a black form sitting in a lounge chair, almost hidden under the olive trees. She could see the blue glow of his eyes when he looked up.

"Are you okay?"

"Yeah, don't mind me. I was listening and lost concentration and knocked over my beer bottle."

Lindy was a bit offended. "Listening to me? Did I bother you?"

"No, no. Nothing like that. I was listening to the trees. They're getting a bit dry. They'll need rain soon."

A lord who listened to trees. How odd! So she asked him how he knew they needed rain. Was it the rustle of dry leaves, or did they talk to him the way animals could talk?

He told her they talked much like the animals did. But very low and very slow. To most lords, their speech was just a low, background hum. White noise. But if they were distressed, they could cry, yell, even scream. She asked a few questions about plants communicating, and he patiently answered them all.

She stopped asking questions, and they were quiet for a long time, sitting in the dark.

Then he spoke again, his voice low and amused. "So, did I bore you to sleep with my tree lecture?"

"No, it's interesting. I'm listening to the trees now. I want to see if I can understand them. Shhh –"

She heard nothing. Then it started to rain, and she heard them, a very faint welcoming noise, a collective "aaahhhh". But

Lindy didn't stay to hear more; she was getting wet, and without another word to the man in the shadows, she left to go to bed.

Lindy and Counsel Kaminska

The EN Embassy in Warsaw was grand. A huge building left over from the old Soviet days, the architecture was as florid as the Stalinist style could be, filled with bas reliefs of massive, sturdy, rather stout farm women leading parades of combines through fields of very neat wheat. The entrance atrium was the size of a football field (at least it seemed that big to Lindy) and filled with massive columns, frescos of old Soviet glories and factory workers, and elaborate tiled floors. The original architects tried very hard to create a modern, brutalist paean to the common man, but their secret desire was to be a fussy Victorian bourgeoisie banker, and both sides warred with each other. It was all lovingly restored, and the only thing missing from the original design was the hammer and sickle, a symbol the present-day Poles were happy to leave in the past.

Lindy was still in her red uniform when she met Counsel Kaminska, an intense, very thin bird of a woman, a human, who shook her hand a little too long and stared a little too fixedly into Lindy's eyes. Maybe she was checking out her glow to make sure she really was a lord and the English weren't sending her faulty goods. In any case, she was very happy to have a lord assigned to her embassy (Even before the Ukrainians had their own personal lord!) and an Elemental to boot. The uniform would change, she was told, when Lord Aethelind accepted the assignment and started working full-time.

"I understand you were born in Poland! We must take you on a visit to your birth home!" The Counsel and her staff were gathered in a reception room to welcome the new lord, and she guided Lindy to the buffet herself, making sure the lord's plate was piled up. "You have to try this! And this!" Lords ate a lot, and she wasn't going to have anyone say they didn't feed theirs well.

Lindy smiled and shook her head. "I was born in 1590, and I have no idea which little village back then was my home. I don't remember its name."

Kaminska stopped and stared. That detail didn't come up in the briefing! She started to do the math and then recovered. "Goodness, I forgot that lords can live so long! Of course, wars and politics have changed the map many times over four hundred years. Poland has always been a battleground for other people's wars." She looked at Lindy, and if she had been a lord herself, her eyes would have glowed bright, "And that is why, Lord Aethelind, I and all these people you see here work and support the Elf Nation. Not just because of the elves, although they are wonderful, but because we work for our own security, too. Russia has been a bad neighbour for centuries. We work for peace for everyone."

The meeting went well, Lindy met the staff and the elves who worked there, and it was an easy decision to accept the assignment and start her duties there. Just like at the London Embassy, she worked four days a week, porting there in the morning and coming home around five, meeting local and regional delegations, school children, church groups, and whoever the EN and the Counsel thought it would be helpful to butter up.

She was assigned a personal elf, a sort of warrior/porter/secretary. Her name was Andrea, and she was of the Warsaw clan. She was Lindy's personal bodyguard, a really formidable woman in every way, and from the moment they met, they doted on each other. Every morning, Andrea would port to the circus tent on Aelfeham House's front lawn and wait for Lindy to walk in (or port in if she was lazy or it was raining), and she'd port her to the Embassy. She kept Lindy's diary, reminded her about appointments, and gave her background briefings on who she was meeting that day. And if anything violent happened, she'd die for her. Andrea was the perfect Girl Friday.

The Green Man

The woman's name was Lord Aethelind, but everyone called her Lindy. He found that out from Lord Jack. She never told him her name, and she never asked his.

Most nights, rain and shine, Ayu would sit in the dark and listen to the world. During the day, he studied with a wide variety of experts, fascinating human men and women who talked about their research in everything from global weather patterns to the dangers of monoculture and the challenges of food security. Most of what they said wasn't new and certainly wasn't surprising, but every day he learned some interesting fact, some new nugget of information, and each day brought a surprise.

Ayu was very happy with his studies, and if the world had been in balance the way he'd left it, he would have been thrilled. But he was starting to understand that by being so out of balance, the new supremacy of the humans had allowed them to flourish intellectually, and that was a gift to be promoted. He was glad he didn't just wipe them out with another ice age when he first woke up and discovered what a mess everything had become.

He could have told the elves and lords to go underground for a decade or two and then solved the entire orc/human problem with one good ecological catastrophe, but that would have created another imbalance, and he was happy he hadn't been tempted by the easy solution. It also would have been very hard on the animals, and some were teetering on extinction now anyway.

So he sat on the terrace every night, rain or shine, to listen to the world and think about what he'd learned that day and mull over different scenarios that would put the world back to rights.

He had time to think before he acted, and, in cosmic time, taking a few months or even a few decades to plan just the right approach was nothing. Acting impulsively without thinking things through was what had caused all the problems in the first place.

Now and then, Lord Aethelind would come to the terrace and sit in the dark. Ayu would listen to her come on her soft feet, and she would sit and say nothing except to the housekeeper elf, who would ask if she wanted for anything and then a thank-you when he brought it.

She didn't greet him when she came and just sat curled up in her chair on the far side of the terrace and looked at the stars, and enjoyed the quiet. Sometimes she knit. But if he said something to her, she answered back and never seemed irritated by his interruptions.

They had conversations, if you could call them that. Short ones, usually triggered by something happening on the terrace. A fragrant bush, and they'd talk about flower scents; a bit of rain, and they'd talk about weather patterns; a bird call, and that was another wide-ranging topic of conversation. She asked intelligent questions and seemed interested in his mini-lectures. Then, after an hour or so, she'd get up and leave, never saying goodbye or making any fuss. She'd just leave.

Over time, they talked about other things. Human politics, what a lord was, why the world started off with one huge continent and why Ayu had split it up like a pie, whether pterodactyls were really an evolutionary mistake or not. They debated a long time over that one, and she held her ground that they were ridiculous. It was fun.

He started to miss her when she didn't come.

He wondered what she looked like.

Lindy and Andrea

After Lindy started working in Warsaw, Paulo would meet her for lunch there. For the first time, she wondered why she didn't see him at night, too. He didn't hang around the TV room like the other single guys, and she didn't see him at the raucous card games that Judy hosted. She guessed that by the end of the day, he was really tired out from his work.

Not that she needed another man sniffing around her when she was not in her room. That's why she went to the terrace, to get away from them for an hour or two if they started to get on her nerves.

She knew the man in the corner was Lord Ayu; she'd figured that out the first night. Maria told her he went out there to meditate and rest, and he didn't want to be bothered, and Lindy absolutely understood that. She didn't want to bother him either, but since he didn't leave, she didn't think he minded if she just sat there for a bit if she was quiet. So she didn't speak until she was spoken to and tried to be polite and respect his space.

But when he said something, she was fine with the conversation; he was really interesting. He knew a lot and didn't talk down to her. He didn't show off, just talked. And, miracles of miracles, he never talked about himself. Between Paulo, Zahn, and the handful of other guys, she was learning enough guy trivia to last her a dozen lord lifetimes. She had a strong feeling Lord Ayu would never tell her how many one-handed push-ups he could do.

Paulo came to lunch, and, like every other time, he was charming, told her a funny story to make her laugh, they talked about the new German Chancellor who was in the news, and then when lunch was over he ported back to his office in Ukraine. But he left behind his beret, and now he was out of uniform, something he was rather particular about. So, because she didn't have a meeting for another hour, she called Andrea.

"Andrea, could you please port me to the node that Paulo uses by his office? I'm going to take his hat back."

Andrea gave her a funny look. She didn't say no; she would never do that. Lords' order, elves obey, but she hesitated. "Why don't you just let me handle this, Lord Lindy. You can take a rest. Can I bring you some more pączki?"

Lindy laughed. "I just finished lunch! I don't need to rest. Actually, I need to get out and move a bit. Just port me. Once I get there, I'll find him. You wait for me at the node. I won't be long."

"Yes, ma'am." Andrea did as she was told. But she wasn't happy.

Lindy walked to the reception desk at the Ukraine node, and the woman at the computer jumped up. The navy-blue uniform with epaulettes did that to some people.

"Hello, I'm Lord Aethelind, and I'm looking for Lord Paulo. Can you please direct me to where he's working today?"

The woman looked up his location on her computer. She was apologetic. "He's in the middle of a big exercise now. Do you mind waiting a bit? He'll be free in about an hour."

Smiling, Lindy shook her head, "No, I have a meeting of my own I have to get back to. I was just going to give him back his beret. He left it at the Warsaw Embassy."

"Oh, I can take care of that. His wife is free; she works down the hall; she can come around and get it for him."

Lindy smiled, handed over the hat, and thanked the receptionist. Back at the node, she nodded to Andrea, and they ported back to the Embassy.

She walked down the hall so fast the elf had to run to keep up. Then Lindy ducked into an empty side office, slammed the door, and rounded on the elf in full flame-eyed lord fury. Andrea stared back into the glowing eyes of the incandescent lord, and she alternated between terror and misery. Terror was fast winning the emotional race, though. A half second later, terror was the clear winner.

"How long have you known, Andrea?"

Oh fuck. She knew. The elf squirmed, groaned, and looked for an escape route.

Andrea looked at her feet; the elf knew what the lord was getting at.

"Two days, Lord Lindy. When he got mad at me for confirming lunch with you. I wanted to find out why he didn't want to be contacted at work."

Lindy didn't say anything, just glared, so Andrea continued. "He married a human about a year ago, not long after he started working there. Private Ukrainian Orthodox ceremony. He never told anyone at the EN."

Andrea started to cry. "I'm sorry, I didn't know what to do. I didn't know if you knew. I was trying to find out if it was public knowledge or not before I brought it up with you. I mean, if you look in the interoffice phone book, she's listed as married to him! I think his wife put that in there, but no one in his chain of command noticed. Probably no one ever tried to contact him; he's not an important lord. I didn't want to mess up his job with the EN, and I didn't want to mess up any relationship you had with him. You'll live forever. What if you two just decided to wait it out?"

Andrea began sobbing. Oh, stars, she was in so much trouble! "When Lord James and Lord Kyrylo find out, they're going to be really mad. They're always telling the male lords to keep their peckers in their pants. When they find out he's been courting a lord and has a human wife on the side, they'll blow up. They both had human wives, Lord Lindy, but they didn't go courting lords until the human women were long gone."

Lindy bent down and glared at Andrea, absolutely beside herself. "And what if I had bonded? And then found out I had a two-timer for a bond-husband. I could bond, and he'd just hold his breath and get the best of both worlds! If he'll cheat on his human wife, he'll cheat on me. Keeping that information to yourself didn't do me any favours, Andrea."

Andrea nodded and just cried harder.

Lindy looked at the elf and then around the room, and she could have screamed. Instead, she kicked a chair and sent it flying to the end of the room. She screamed anyway. Andrea flinched.

"Look. I'm really, really mad. At you. Me. Him. I'm going to need some time to cool down. That's just the way it is."

"I'll quit, Lord Lindy. I know I've screwed up bad. I didn't know what to do. If an orc came at you, I'd know what to do: I'd chop off his head. But someone you're bonking – I didn't know. I didn't want to screw up your life, and I ended up screwing up your life. I'm really sorry."

"Oh, you're lucky; you didn't screw up my life." Lindy was cooling down. "I wasn't in love with him, but I liked him, and now I'm – upset, really upset. Humiliated. We were meeting for lunch, and everyone saw that. People at home think I'm dating him, maybe even sleeping with a married man. How many knew he was married? He must think I'm so stupid. And we never *bonked.* I haven't even kissed him. It never got that far."

Lindy was in tears. All the remaining anger fizzed out like a popped balloon, and she deflated into a chair at the conference table. "I'm pretty clueless when it comes to men. I'm not a virgin, Andrea, but I might as well be one. Paulo must have figured that out from day one. He didn't have to lie to me; I'm just totally clueless." She let out a great shuddering sigh.
"I'm so stupid –"

The elf just stood there, the picture of misery. They hadn't been working together for very long, but now she was going to be fired from her dream job, and she deserved it.

"I have to trust you, Andrea."

"Yes, ma'am." The elf sighed, waiting for it. She was going to be fired.

"If you learn *anything* that worries you and will affect me, you have to tell me, no matter how unpleasant or embarrassing. You have to promise me that. Don't overthink it. Don't wait."

"Yes, ma'am."

Lindy sighed. "Okay, let's get back to work then."

And the lord turned, walked back out in the hall, and went to the next appointment.

Andrea couldn't believe it. She wasn't fired!

Lord Lindy didn't talk to the elf all afternoon, but at three, during a break, she asked Andrea if there was a way to block her schedule from other people's phones. So they couldn't track her.

Andrea said she didn't know, but she would look into it. Lindy nodded and simply said, "Get him blocked from seeing where I am. I don't care who you need to talk to. If they ask why, tell them the truth."

At four thirty, when she was stepping out of the shower, Lindy had an urgent call alert blinking on her phone. It wasn't Paulo; it was Lord James.

He didn't dance around and bluntly asked her if the information he'd received was true – that Lord Paulo had been courting her, she found out he was married, and now she didn't want any further contact with him.

She said yes, she had been told by the receptionist at the Ukraine transport node that he was married to someone who worked there. The woman didn't even have to look it up. Lindy said she had been under the impression he was single, and she didn't want to continue her friendship with him because she didn't think it was appropriate.

"I thought we were having lunch dates. He never mentioned his wife, but then –" Lindy had to stop for a second. "He never said he was single either. None of my girlfriends here knew he was married. If any of the guys did, they didn't say anything, and I think they would have."

Lord James was silent.

"You didn't bond, I hope."

"No, no bonding. I didn't even sleep with him. It never got that far."

There was a sigh of relief at his end.

"Okay, don't worry about this. He won't contact you, but if he does, you need to call me directly. Don't hesitate. Take care of yourself, Lord Aethelind."

She thanked him and hung up. More humiliation. Now her idiocy was known at the highest levels. Just as she put down the phone, there was a knock at the door.

Lindy almost didn't open it, but she did. She didn't want to talk to Paulo. She didn't even want to see his face.

Rita, Talia, Maria, Alizah, Althea, Sarah, Vrt, and Judy – her whole sisterhood – were there. They had a shitload of pizza, too many bottles of wine to count, and a big box of tissues.

They sat on her bed, ate pizza, drank too much wine, and talked about the perfidy of men all night.

Paulo

The GSN found out about Paulo's human wife at four o'clock, just as Lindy was porting back from her eventful day at work, when five grim elves entered his room and cleaned it out. When a passerby asked what was going on, they told him. Lord Paulo was moving out of Aelfeham House permanently and moving in with his human wife in Ukraine. He had been married for over a year and hadn't told anyone.

That nugget of information took about fifteen minutes to make the rounds. Then the GSN found that not a single female lord of any status or age was visible on Paulo's schedule, and he was invisible on theirs. He was wiped from social or professional contact with any Aelfeham House female. He could talk to his male friends, and a few of them called him and wanted to know what the hell was going on, but those phone calls died out pretty quickly.

After Gary's attempted bond-rape of Freyja, the community became even more unforgiving when it came to cads. Even though Paulo begged, screamed, and whined to anyone who listened that *nothing had happened*, his friends still thought he was a jerk and didn't want anything to do with him. He said he and Lindy were just friends. Buddies. Mates. He wasn't trying to date her. She wasn't even his type.

He skipped over the little detail that he'd kept his marriage hidden, a lie by omission. He'd wanted to keep his options open.

The next day, all of the lords had a directive from Lord Cadence. Lords who fell in love and married a human must notify the EN. There was no ban on marrying a human or having a human lover past the three-day rule, but everything had to be out in the open. She emphasised that bonding was permanent and sometimes involuntary, so understanding everyone's status was only fair and right to all parties, including the humans involved.

Like a lot of bureaucratic emails belabouring the obvious, even though names weren't named, everyone knew what was going on.

The Green Man and the Fortuneteller

Ayu heard about Lord Aethelind's public embarrassment when he read Lord Cadence's email and asked his housekeeper elf about it. Again, the subject matter cut a bit too close to the quick for him to just scroll past it, and he wondered if this had anything to do with him.

But no, this was about Lord Aethelind.

The elf was indignant. Lord Lindy didn't do anything wrong, but Lord Paulo had been wooing her, and he already had a wife. Yeah, she was just a human, but she existed, and he didn't tell Lord Lindy. It wasn't so bad that he had a wife, but it was really bad that he'd lied and led the lord on. Poor Lord Lindy, her heart was broken. It was a good thing she'd never bonded with Lord Paulo!

Ayu was upset, probably more than he should have been and probably – no, certainly – because the entire incident between Lindy and Paulo uncomfortably paralleled his.

He had a dozen excuses about why he had his fling. His and Gaia's relationship cooled, she took him for granted, Gaia manipulated him, and on and on. Her bonding with him without talking to him about it first was a barbed-wire lasso that always chafed. But in the end, it was a combination of cowardice and laziness that made him behave dishonourably, and that wasn't an excuse at all.

If Ayu had read a Victorian novel about a woman who got pregnant to trap a man and force him to marry her, he would have recognised the pattern right away. But in Lord Aethelind's romance novel, she was the innocent party, fooled by the rake who had a wife hidden in another town.

Ayu stayed with Gaia too long. He knew that if he left her, she would suffer, so he muddled through for years, putting off her pain and telling himself it was because he didn't want to see her hurt when it was all really because he was a coward. Done right, reversing a bond was risky but possible. It meant going into a cauldron and having your body reset. It was very public and painful, especially if one of the parties didn't want to un-bond.

If Gaia had been a troublesome island that needed some tough-love terraforming to get it back to health, he wouldn't have hesitated. But she was a woman he'd once loved, so he found a side piece, and when Gaia discovered her and made a fuss, he stomped off in a pout and told himself it was her fault.

Ayu wasn't proud of that.

That night, as he sat in the dark and listened to the world, he thought about how two people's private moments affected the public world. Two parents split up, and their children are scarred, the wider family is upset and mortified, and life goes to shit. It can take years for everyone to get back on an even keel. He and Gaia had an argument and split up, and the world was upended, and millions died. It would take centuries to bring back balance.

He took a sip of his beer and sighed. Then he heard her, the soft little feet.

She walked to her chair, and in an instant, the housekeeper elf was there with a blanket and a big cup of something hot. It smelled like mulled wine.

He let her settle in. What to say? How's it going? What's up? All those questions would just remind her of her heartbreak.

No question then. Just a statement. "You haven't been here for a couple of days."

A long silence; did that really need an answer? It was just a statement of fact.

"Yes, I've been lying low, thinking about things."

"That's what I do every night. Lay low and think about things."

"What do you think about?"

Ayu thought about thinking, which made him smile. "I think about worlds. I think about this world and how I get too worried about the details and forget the big picture."

"Details?"

"Yeah, idiotic, little things. Stuff that only lasts a day. I get all wound up about one corner of one field on one day and obsess over it and forget that it's part of a huge whole. I think it's because I only see that one stupid moment in time and study it to death. I need to step back, let go of the bad, ugly bits, and look at the beautiful whole. But it's hard to do."

"Yeah, it's hard to let go of stupid shit. I nurse my mistakes." Her voice cracked, but she steadied. "But you say you obsess over little things; how is that even possible? You worry about huge things. Whole forests. Entire species. Continents. How can anything be little to you?"

He chuckled. "It's all a matter of scale. I worry about large things if you compare them to the size of lords, but everything is a small part of something else. Sometimes we need to see the whole, and it's not possible. I sit and think about forests, but maybe that's because I've never seen the whole Earth. And the Earth is just a tiny mote, an atom in the universe."

He looked at the sky. "It's all a matter of balance. Little bumps seem important, and then we put them in perspective, and they're not important at all. Big things are easy to ignore because they overwhelm us, and we put them out of our minds because it's too hard to face them."

Lindy looked at the stars. Ayu obviously knew all about her public embarrassment over Paulo, and he was absolutely right; it was nothing in the big scheme of things. Her friends didn't mock or pity her; they were angry. When she was kicked down, they offered their hands and picked her up, and every time she thought of them standing at her door holding pizza, she choked up. Their friendship was the big thing she should remember. She had lost a lover she hadn't wanted in the first place, and she'd found a sisterhood of friends and a clan that pulled together to support her.

She had done nothing wrong; her natural caution wouldn't permit her to do anything more than eat lunch with Paulo. She wasn't heartbroken, not at all, just hurt that a man she liked and was starting to trust had taken advantage of her. She was embarrassed that she had been gulled. The Romani made an art of gulling the gadjo, and here the gadjo had gulled her. Thank god she didn't have a moment of weakness, an attack of lust like she had with David.

Ayu, who had probably seen everything on this Earth at least ten times, didn't judge her as a gullible fool and, in his roundabout way, was trying to make her feel better. Keep things in perspective, he said. He was a friend, too, and was trying to support her. Lindy felt better already.

Ayu took a sip of his beer. This conversation wasn't going to help her at all. He changed tack.

"So, Lord Aethelind, what's important to you? What's a big thing in your life?"

Lindy looked at the lord, a black silhouette in his chair. He sat very still, watching her, the faintest glint of moonlight shining off the bottle in his hand, his eyes glowing like two blue fireflies.

No one had ever asked what was important to her. She'd never asked that of herself. She didn't know how to answer.

"I don't know. All of my life, I've worried about surviving to the next day. Looking at the big picture wasn't even on my to-do list. I guess just being happy is a good goal. Being safe, that's a big one. I can't be happy if I'm not safe."

His voice was incredulous, and he regretted what he said the minute it left his mouth. "You're a lord! You're a powerful one, too, from the feel of it. How can you ever worry about your safety!"

Of course, thousands of lords had died from Gaia's temper tantrum when he was off sulking, asleep. It was a stupid question.

She laughed, peals of genuine laughter. "Oh, dear – you need to read about the witch hunts! The Nazis! Everything in between! You're so powerful that you don't have to worry about anything! Me? Every time I turn around, someone's trying to kill me just because of who I am. You're an elephant, a whale! I'm a shrimp."

"You're not a shrimp, not at all!"

"Okay, I'm not a shrimp. I'm a wasp. I have a sting, but I'm still small, and a lucky swat will kill me." She chuckled and took a sip of her wine.

She told him her story. How she was born in 1590, stolen, enslaved and surviving through two hundred years of witch hunts and wars.

"Europe was one continuous battleground! I've passed through so many warring armies, I can't remember them all. I've driven my wagon through fields and fields of corpses. And each war killed more and more people, civilians and soldiers. World War II killed twenty million in Europe – men, women, and children. The Nazi's tried to exterminate my human clan, the Roma. They tried to exterminate me."

She paused. "Then, for seventy-five years – a tiny slice of time – I was safe. If I hid my ears and if I pretended I was something else, if I lived alone, I could live. As hard as they tried, the Nazi's couldn't put me in a prison, but if I made one of my own, I could live. Then it all started up again. The witch hunts. I survived, though. I escaped one more time and came here."

Ayu didn't know what to say. "I hope, Lord Aethelind, you'll always be safe here."

"Oh, I love it here! From what I've heard, you have no idea what it's like to not have to pretend you're something else just to survive and to be accepted for what you are. Did you ever hide from anything, Lord Ayu? You're older than dirt, but in all that time, did anyone ever hunt you? Try to kill you?

I have friends here. For the first time in my life, there are people who know me and think I'm just fine the way I am. There are storm clouds on the horizon. I've lived through too many wars not to recognise the signs, but I'm not going to sleep through the warning sirens [this made Ayu wince, but he knew she wasn't referring to him]. I'll fight for what the elves and the lords have built here."

Then, abruptly, she stood up, a black shadow in the dark. "I've talked too much. I've told myself I would respect your desire to be left alone, and I haven't done that. I'll blame the wine. Thanks for letting me talk." And she walked away.

He sat for a few minutes, absorbing what she'd said. She was right. He'd never lived in fear. No one had ever tried to kill him. All she wanted was to be safe and live a happy life. It wasn't too much to ask.

Lindy

When Lindy saw Andrea the next morning, she asked her to find a poster, one she had seen of a photograph of the Earth taken by astronauts from space. An easy assignment and one the elf did with dispatch, a few taps on her tablet, a double check that it was the correct photo, and she was done. It would be in her room, Andrea said, when Lord Lindy got home that night.

She and Andrea went to work, walking down the long, echoing halls from the porting room to the front door, Andrea trotting beside Lindy, telling her the schedule of the day and details about the tours.

The first tour was a class of eight-year-olds coming to see elves and lords working and to learn how they lived. Lord Cadence loved these tours; she said they were developing good relations with the next generation while the children were still open to new ideas. Soon, there would be many humans who had never lived in a world without elves and lords and couldn't imagine a world without them. Many had probably seen elves before, in the markets and around the villages, but Lindy would be the first lord these children had met in person.

The big atrium was full, and elves and human employees bustled about, each looking busier than the last. Through the door, Lindy could see the class walking up the wide steps, some of the kids jumping up and down on the steps and playing as kids do, and as they entered the doorway, Lindy smiled and walked to the teacher –

She had no future.

Lindy screamed, "Andrea! Port!" The elf made a port, but instead of Lindy running through it as they had practised in an emergency, the lord swept the stunned and screaming children into it with her ability, en masse, like they were plates.

The teacher's head exploded.

Lindy threw herself to the side. There was a hail of bullets; one hit her forearm, but by some miracle, she scrambled back through the door and cowered behind a huge column, her heart beating so hard it was going to burst from her chest. The roar of battle in the atrium was deafening, the thunderclap of gunshots everywhere, people screaming, and the sound of elves porting in and out rattled like castanets.

Then she heard a voice. He was yelling in Russian.

"THE LORD! We want the demon LORD!"

There was a scuffle, and to her left, Lindy saw Warrior Elves pop in behind the shooters, a lightning sweep of their swords decapitating three of them, and then they winked out. Lindy risked a second glance around the column and saw two more shooters dressed like maintenance workers. They had chokeholds on two hostages, human women who worked the reception desk, and the terrorists held guns to their heads. Pressed up against a wall with the huge reception desk as a rampart to hold off the elves, the gunmen were barricaded in, and the elves couldn't port in behind them.

"ANDREA!" The elf found the lord and ported to her.

"Lord Lindy, port out *now*!" Andrea hissed.

"No. Wait." Lindy stripped off her coat, took the elf knife out of her boot, and with one clean swipe sliced off her braid. She'd never used the knife before; it was just a decorative part of her uniform, and she was lucky she didn't cut herself. But then, where was that blood coming from?

"Take these and port across the room. Wave them at them. Make them think this coat is me. Give me a second – just a second to have a clean look at them."

"Lor –"

"*Do it!* Direct order, Andrea! Do it! Oh, and don't die. Direct order."

The elf grimaced, screamed in frustration and ported out.

Then she heard Andrea.

"HERE I AM! DON'T KILL THEM! I –"

Lindy looked around the column and saw the shooters take their pistols from the necks of their hostages and aim their guns at the lord's jacket with her trademark braid –

She ripped their fucking heads off.

For one long second, time stood still; there was complete silence.

Then it was chaos again. Soldiers ported in, so many that they could hardly move. Warrior Elves everywhere. People crying and screaming. Ambulances and medics yelling as they tended to the wounded.

Andrea blinked back to Lindy's column. "Will you go *now*! PLEASE!" and Lindy let her port her all the way to the node at Aelfeham House.

Andrea couldn't leave the transport node, she was a Warsaw Clan elf and *terrior* didn't permit that, so Lindy hugged her and thanked her. There were already healer elves trying to get the lord on a stretcher, but she wouldn't bother with that. She walked to her room, the healer bandaged up her arm, and she fell on her bed, fully clothed, and passed out.

The Aftermath

Four people died, not including the five terrorists. The teacher died with the first shot, and when Lindy dove to the floor, three people inside the atrium were hit by stray bullets. By the time the terrorists forced their way inside, most of the workers had been cleared out by elves, but the two receptionists nearest the door were grabbed by the terrorists. After Lindy pulled off their captors' heads, the women were treated for shock and some scrapes.

Two of the kids had broken bones from the force of Lindy's push as they shot through the port. Andrea had opened a port to a panic room deep in the embassy, so that's where they ended up.

No elves died or were injured.

The terrorists were Russian nationals who had immigrated to Poland in '22 when Putin started the Russian War against Ukraine. They'd posed as refugees and had integrated into Polish society for years, but, as seen in interviews worldwide, their neighbours had no idea who lived amongst them. They seemed like really nice people. Very quiet. Minded their own business.

When the new lord was placed in the Warsaw embassy, someone in Russia activated the cell with the idea that killing a lord would strike terror in the rest of the lords and weaken the faith the Europeans had in the EN. The new Warsaw lord was a woman, and all she could do was move plates around. She was an easy target. It would be a show of Russian will and power.

It didn't work.

The elves hung the heads of the five terrorists on the Russian side of the Wall. The Russians tried to pull them down (they were bad for morale), but it took three days of orc and human meat waves to get them before the EN got tired of killing Russians and let them have the rotting skulls.

The Green Man

She was fine, the housekeeper elf assured him. Just a minor flesh wound on her lower arm, almost at her wrist, and with elf medicine, there wouldn't even be a scar when it healed.

No scars? Ayu just stared at the elf. No scars? How could there not be scars?

The night before, all Lord Aethelind said she wanted was to live in safety and peace, and the very next morning, five people had tried to assassinate her. She had told him that every single day of her life, she had to defend against someone trying to kill her because of what she was, and in a place of safety, they tried it again. He thought she was exaggerating for effect; her life wasn't that perilous, was it? Obviously, she wasn't exaggerating at all.

No scars?

Ayu was deeply, profoundly shocked. The risks the present-day lords faced were theoretical yesterday. Today, it hit him in the face with a sledgehammer. In his vast life Before Times, no one tried to kill lords, and there were no wars between nation-states because there were no nation-states. A political assassination was inconceivable because the only leaders were Gaia and the Council. Oh, orcs and humans had their frictions and insanities, but that's what Warrior Lords were for, and it took less than a thousand of them to police the entire world.

What monstrous world had he woken up to?

He didn't even know what she looked like, but the very idea of Lindy being shot – it was unthinkable. The idea that she could have died was unbearable.

No scars? Her arm might not be scarred, but his psyche certainly was. How could hers not be?

He asked the elf where she was, and the housekeeper told him she was in her room, sleeping. She'd used a lot of magic and, of course, the stress was exhausting. But she'd be okay soon. She'd probably be up for dinner.

Normally, Ayu ate in his rooms. He had a nice flat with a very large dining table in it, and he liked to read and look at maps when he had dinner. The Green Man knew all about the Breakfast Room, but he wasn't there to socialise; he was there to study, and he seldom went to the communal dining room.

He thought about going there tonight for dinner and then changed his mind. He didn't trust himself to be calm, and besides, there was one small detail that held him back.

He still didn't know what she looked like.

Lindy

Dinner was a celebration of life. Of survival. Of respect.

When Lindy walked into the Breakfast Room for dinner, the place erupted. Everyone was there, even those who usually didn't eat dinner with the group, and they all wanted to hug her, to touch her, to tearfully ask her if she was okay and tell her how glad they were that she was.

The Warrior Lords all stood up and bowed to her, which made Lindy blush and the rest of the room clap.

It all turned into quite a party.

By ten, Lindy had had enough and begged off and went back to her room to sleep, which everyone understood, and the party began to break up. While a few diehards stayed until the wee hours of the morning, most had jobs and places to be the next day, and while they celebrated, their enemies worked and planned their next atrocity.

At twelve, Lindy's alarm went off, and she dressed and walked to the terrace to see if Lord Ayu was there. He was sitting in his chair, and there was a moon tonight, and Lindy could see his white beard and hair catching bits of moonlight.

"I was hoping you'd be here! I was afraid the crowd in the Breakfast Room would put you off."

And suddenly she was off the ground, her feet dangling, and she couldn't breathe because he was hugging her so hard. He didn't kiss her, just buried his face in her neck, and for a second she thought he was crying. She felt him shudder, but when he finally set her down, his voice was even.

He took a deep breath. "I am so glad you're alright. When I heard about the attack –"

Lindy had to step back. Attack? Oh, yeah, that thing. That was a lifetime ago. This morning. All she could think of now was how he smelled. A minute ago, she couldn't breathe, and now all she wanted to do was gulp in his scent.

She took another step back. "Yeah. Well. It was pretty bad when it was going on, but I survived. I always do."

He could almost see her in the moonlight. Her huge eyes glowed bright, and the rims of her ears caught the moon's reflected sunbeams. She had beautiful ears.

"They hurt you!"

"I got nicked on my wrist. It'll heal." Then she sighed. "I had to cut off my hair, though, and I had nice hair. It'll grow back."

He stepped forward and put his hand behind her head and ruffled her hair. The elves had trimmed and styled it so it didn't look chopped off, but now it was really short.

"You had a very long braid. I saw it whenever you walked back into the house. Why is it gone?"

And she explained about the subterfuge. She'd cut off her braid to fool the attackers into thinking she was somewhere she wasn't.

"Clever woman! It'll grow back; a worthwhile loss if it kept you alive."

He didn't remove his hand; he was standing too close, and Lindy started getting scent-drunk again. She giggled. "Oh, it's not lost. I still have it! For some reason, the elves brought it back when they brought back my jacket."

"They wouldn't keep it. A female lord's hair has immeasurable value. It has magic, and if you know what to do, it can heal and make things grow. Healer elves use it to stitch wounds up." he was still stroking the back of her neck. Then his fingertips moved to her earlobe, her jawline. It was hypnotic.

"Then you can have it. I don't know what to do with it, and you make things grow. Maybe it will help in some way." Then she shivered and, with a huge effort, stepped back again and broke his hold on her. She couldn't think and had to get out of there before she did something stupid – like kiss him.

"But here – the reason I came looking for you was to give you a real gift, not a hank of hair. You said you didn't know what the Earth looked like," and she shoved the cardboard tube at Ayu and ran to the door.

"What is it!" he yelled, and she stopped at the doorway and, for the first time, she turned as she left, her face bathed in the hall light. She was laughing. She was absolutely gorgeous.

"Open it up! I've given you the world." And she spun around and ran off.

The Orc

The orc sniper, hidden in an old trench leftover from the Russian War, looked up at the top of the Wall and, through his scope, saw the heads of three men silhouetted against the bright Ukrainian sky. There was a flash, a reflection of the sun on a pair of binoculars. He knew they would only stay visible for a second, and it was only by the most outrageous chance of sheer dumb luck that he was poised and ready when the heads appeared. He was just adjusting his sights at the time.

But there they were, his sniper rifle with its extended range was loaded and ready, and he took his shot.

The angle was perfect. The timing was perfect. The shot was perfect.

Kyrylo

The bullet entered Kyrylo's good eye.

He was dead.

Caddy

Caddy sat bolt upright at her desk and screamed as if the world was coming to an end.

It was.

The Elves and Lords

The elves and the lords heard the Peace Lord's scream of utter agony, and they knew.

The Fortuneteller

Lindy was in the stables, talking to Old Bob and trying to convince him that the new bridle was going to feel better than the old, broken-in one, when she heard the Primary's scream.

Kyrylo

Kyrylo sat up. He was in a white, sparkly cloud, a nebula, and in front of him was an open door. Without anyone telling him, he knew what had happened and where he was.

He was dead, and the door was the entrance to the Void. Oh, the pull was strong. He had never felt such unbearable despair, such anguish.

He had left Caddy, and now she would die in her own acid pool of agony. Ivana was damaged forever. Rurik would lose another set of parents, another safe haven, and what would that do to him?

The fate of the elves and lords without their primaries was back on the balance, and the scales were tipped against them.

He had lost everything. They had lost everything. Everything.

And in front of him, the Gates to the Void stood open and through them the promise of forgetfulness, rest, calm. Perfection.

All that went through his head in a second. A nanosecond. He didn't so much think it as he just knew it.

Then, in front of the door, appeared a woman. A horrible, ugly, rat-faced, furious woman. A naked mole rat queen with raging green glowing eyes, sitting on a mound of a thousand squirming naked mole rat pups. Jammed in her mouth was a stick, but it didn't stop her from hissing at him.

"It's not your ti –"

The Fortuneteller

Lindy stopped time.

She heard the Primary's scream, she knew Krylylo was dead, and she saw the futures of nine billion people alter and shift, and the horror of it was too much, and she stopped

Time.

She didn't hear the horses shriek as she flamed up in the barn because when she stopped Time, they froze, mid-scream.

It took all she had, every ounce of her being. Almost every ounce; if she used up any more, she'd die herself.

But when you stop Time, you are outside of space and place, too, and she used the last remnant of herself, all she had left, to use her magic gift of moving things to give Kyrylo a shove. A tiny nudge.

That infinitesimal nudge was infinitely heavy because by nudging Kyrylo a centimetre, she nudged and altered the futures of an entire universe, an impossibly complex web of possibilities.

But she nudged; she didn't hesitate because there was no more time.

"My life for his," she whispered to the gods, and she pushed, one last time, as hard as she could.

Lord Aethelind o Devinàtoro, the Fortuneteller, died.

The Green Man

The Green Man fell, all the air knocked out of him. Lindy was dead.

Something had killed her. All the power, all that he had, and he didn't – couldn't – keep her safe.

He pounded the floor with his fists, screaming in utter agony and fury, and on the other side of the world, in an Australian outback, a fissure split the Earth, and in the explosion, a new volcano was born.

Time

There was a jerk, a reordering, and Time moved on. The elves in the Safe Haven and the transport nodes, which were bubbles outside of space and time, were the only ones who heard the Fortuneteller's whisper.

"My life for his."

To the gods, that was a fair trade.

Kyrylo and Caddy

The explosion took out the barn and all of the horses, the four elves, and two humans working in there. There was nothing left but a pile of ash. An entire wall of the Breakfast Room collapsed in the concussion wave, as well as a wing of flats, and while there were injuries, no one in the house died.

On the Wall, Kyrylo was alive because the bullet didn't enter his eye and explode into his brain, but his change of fortune nudged him enough that it grazed the bony orbit of his good eye, taking it out. Within seconds, the Warrior Elves who always surrounded him ported the War Lord to Dr Mandy, who put him in an emergency cauldron as fast as they could get his clothes off.

Norma found Caddy kneeling on the floor of her office, retching and shaking, but when the elves told her Kyrylo was alive and on his way to the cauldron, she pulled herself back together and did what she always did. She managed.

Gaia and Lindy

Gaia was pissed, but, on the other hand, having two visitors of such importance inside of an hour (her hour was not the same as everyone else's) was interesting. It certainly broke up her day!

The woman, the one who was known as Aethelind the Fortuneteller, was still asleep, but she would wake up soon, and she'd have to figure out what to do with her. The Gates were firmly shut for this one, so she wasn't ready for the Void, not yet. But she couldn't stay here with Gaia, either. Not that she wouldn't mind the company, but it would be getting a bit crowded, and no one really liked permanent houseguests. Visitors, yes. Squatters, no.

Gaia looked at the world and knew that she would have a rush going through the doors soon. Those damn orcs! If she had her way, she'd eliminate every last one of them, but the gods dictated balance, not her. She'd learnt that little truth the hard way.

The Fortuneteller woke up, and, after the usual confusion of all those who came to consciousness on the wrong side of the Gates to the Void, she was really quite calm about the whole thing.

She had, after all, freely given her life in trade for the War Lord's life and as deserved punishment for the temerity of stopping Time itself. So to find herself sitting on a cloud of stars and watching the Gatekeeper continually mutate from one form to the next –

Well, death could be worse.

She and Gaia talked. They talked about futures and pasts and the possibility that Time was an entity and not a state. They talked about the problems of leadership, whether it was leading a small band of the weakest humans through the turmoil of their never-ending wars or managing a world of lords, each more powerful than the next, in a continual quest for balance. Gaia talked about hubris and pride and warned Lindy (they were on a first-name basis by then) of the flip side of hubris and the danger of being too humble.

"Balance, child, balance. The hardest thing to do is to be clear-eyed about what you are when everyone is telling you what *they* think you are. I was too prideful, and you, I think, have been too quick to hide who you are. I had too many people telling me I was wonderful, and you had too many telling you how awful you are and trying to kill you. I wasn't that great, and you weren't that bad."

She laughed, thinking about past triumphs. "I cut quite a swath through the field of men, but having every man tell me how beautiful and wonderful I was went to my head. I thought everyone was equally enamoured with my perfection. It turned out not to be true." A shadow passed over her face, a literal storm cloud now. The stick she always held floated in the rain.

"I had dozens of men until I bonded. Your soul has been marked by only one and never bonded to anyone. Why is that?"

Lindy smiled at the she-wolf and watched her turn into a flower, which meant Gaia couldn't talk for a few minutes. No mouth.

"When I was stolen from my parents, I was eight, and for the next seven years, I was a slave. The man who stole me thought that he had a witch because of my eyes, and he was sure I could turn rocks into gold. Oh, did he beat me when he learnt I couldn't do that! But his wife wouldn't let him kill me. I think, in her own way, she grew fond of me. Anyway, I lived with them as a slave, and then one day he came to us and said he'd sold me to pay a debt, and I was to go live with another Roma family."

Lindy looked at her hands. "The new family gave me to their youngest son to keep him happy and so he would stop bothering the girls with families to protect them. He was, they would say now, mentally retarded. Back then, we said he was simple. Very simple. But he looked normal and did as he was told most of the time, but his natural hormones, his lust, weren't held back by any self-control at all. I found that it didn't matter to him how he got release, lying on me or with my hands, and I learned to control him. I kept him clean and fed, and was his concubine, I guess. Wife, nurse, housekeeper, whore."

She grinned, but it wasn't a happy grin.

"Milkmaid. I couldn't escape. As awful as my life was, if I left to join a real community, I'd be burned as a witch the minute my eyes glowed. I saw witches burned and never forgot the lesson. I had no abilities, nothing, because I hadn't grown into them yet, so I had to use my brains. With the pennies his family gave me to keep their son clothed and fed, I saved, traded, and built up a little business as a trader. I sold beads and jewellery. Everyone thought he was the merchant because, as a slave, I had no money and no rights. I wasn't his wife, so I didn't even have that status; I was his property. But I could tell him what to do, and he did exactly what I said.

Then one day I saw a young girl from a good family talking to him, and I realised that she thought he was a catch! Dobil wasn't bad looking, although he disgusted me, but being objective, he was clean, decent looking, and seemed to have some money. So he talked slowly and said stupid things – many men do. I found them in his bed one day, screwing away like rabbits. I knew the path both he and she were taking, but it didn't take my magic to figure that out. Anyone could see how that would end up.

She fell pregnant, and her family insisted that Dobil marry her. They didn't need me, a weird, glow-eyed, totally useless witch, and they certainly didn't want to support another mouth from the money Dobil made. She could take my place in the caravan. They debated selling me on, but in the end, I convinced the girl's family and Dobil that it would be good luck to free me and let me go. So he gave me three silver coins, a mule, and the clothes on my back and said never to contact him again; that was all I was going to get. I think by then they were afraid of me.

I didn't have another man until I met David. For one thing, as I grew older, my eyes and my ears scared them silly, and being a witch in seventeenth-century Europe was a death sentence. So, no man could bed me and see me as I was. But also, I just never met anyone who seemed to like me for myself, and I was never tempted to risk exposure. Men didn't like me; they certainly didn't lust for me. One man told me that when I looked at him, I saw through his soul, and that was terrifying. I knew too much.

I only had one night with David, and it was a lot of fun. But more than that, it was a revelation. A man could share my bed and not run away screaming in fear. Even enjoy me as much as I enjoyed him. But hey, I'm dead now. It limits a girl's dating prospects."

Gaia looked at Lindy and thought *what a sad story*; she wondered if she would have survived if they had traded places. Probably not.

"You'll have a man again, I'm sure of it." Then she grinned, a terrifying grimace on the face of a Halloween goblin. "Has the fortuneteller ever had her fortune told? I'll wager not! What if we make a little trade? I'll read your fortune if you read mine!"

Lindy laughed. "You can't read a lord's fortune! And I can't read a whatever-it-is-you-are's fortune! We have timelines that are too long, too obscure and tangled, and too much in control of the stars to read."

Gaia harrumphed. "You're not in Kansas any more, Dorothy. The rules you had down there don't apply up here. Make an old woman happy; I don't get much entertainment up here. Will you take the trade?"

The Fortuneteller shrugged and agreed. What could they lose? Gaia was insisting, and it would pass the time.

She looked at the ever-mutating Gatekeeper, and her eyes glowed bright as she studied the possibilities. There was only one line; there were no offshoots. Gaia was going to pass through the door to the Void, but the Fortuneteller had no idea when. She told Gaia what she saw, and amazingly, the woman started crying.

"Hope – you've given me hope! I started this –" and she waved her fifteen-fingered hand,

" – job when I killed myself. The Nameless Lord did it before I came here, passed through the Gates, and left me here. But how do I finish? When do I finish? Will I ever finish, or am I stuck here, mutating and atoning for my unforgivable sins forever? I don't know what I have to do to balance my evil on Earth, so telling me that one day I'll move to the Void means that I will do something, and one day my time here will be done. It's a great comfort to know that the gods will one day forgive me and let me pass through the door. A great comfort."

After some sniffling, she sat back and smiled at Lindy. Her turn. Gaia read Lindy's fortune by throwing some chicken bones, and they landed on the cloud with an incongruous clatter. Smiling, she looked at the bones, and then her eyes snapped with green fire. She looked up at the Fortuneteller with a hundred eyes bright from a boiling stew of emotions. Fear, jealousy, sorrow, rage –

– and then she disappeared.

Goodness, thought Lindy, that didn't go well! Gaia saw something awful, and for a minute, Lindy wondered if she was going to end up as the demi-god's replacement. Maybe she was already.

But Gaia popped back in, her basilisk eyes red-rimmed, but her face calm. "Sorry, that was emotional of me. I shouldn't have made that barter, not at all. Hubris on my part, once again. You said not to do it, and I insisted." She sighed. "I always know better."

She gulped and told the fortune. "You'll go back to Earth and have a long, long, forever life. A happy life. I can't see how far forever is, but it will dwarf mine, I feel that. Soon you'll find a man who will love you until the end of time." She hesitated. "When you find him, I want you to give him this." And she handed Lindy her stick.

"That's a lovely fortune, Gaia; I couldn't ask for more. I'm sorry if it upset you."

"Oh, I'm not – Well, I *am* a bit jealous, but that's my problem, isn't it?" She started to fade. "The stick is magic; it will help you get through any troubles on the way to your forever man. When you meet him, just give him the stick, and he'll know what to do with it. That will help me up here, and completing that task will repay any debt to me. You must go now."

"Thank y –"

And the Fortuneteller was gone.

Gaia looked at the space where the Fortuneteller once sat, bitter tears running down her turtle cheeks. "No need to thank me. I have my own debts to settle, and you will pay one for me."

Caddy

There was no one in the room; she had sent them all out.

The minute the door closed, Caddy sank to the floor in front of the cauldron, sobbing her eyes out, giving herself the luxury of emotional release before she had to return to calm, steady, mother, wife, Queen of the Fairies, Leader of the Elf Nation, Cadence Miller Aeldor Melnyk.

In the last hour, her world had flipped inside out and back again.

Kyrylo had died. Then he was alive.

Lord Aethelind was alive. Then she died.

"My life for his."

Everyone knew what had happened; the elves who were, for whatever reason, in a transport node or in the Safe Haven and so outside of space and time, all heard her cry to the gods. Everyone – lords and elves – felt the War Lord come back and felt the gaping hole the Fortuneteller left when the barn exploded from her magic.

Adem said she stopped Time. If anyone would recognise such immense power, he could. He was in hysterics, clinging to Malachi for dear life, and all Malachi could do was hold him and let him cry it out. She stopped *Time,* he kept saying, over and over.

Lord Ayu was in shock. Some of the elves thought he was gradually bonding to Aethelind. They talked almost every night, the elves said. He was courting her. Or maybe she was courting him. It was hard to tell. They even had bets up in the Safe Haven, and the odds were good.

Lord Aethelind survived the terrorists by just one day, only to die, if indirectly, by their hands the next.

Lord Aethlind had given herself so that the elves and lords could have a fighting chance at surviving the coming onslaught with an intact leadership. She had stopped Time and, in that space, bargained with the gods, two bonded lords for the price of one. *"My life for his."*

And they agreed to the trade. She was worth two bonded Primaries.

Because of Aethelind, Kyrylo was alive. And because Kyrylo was alive, so was Caddy.

Mandy said she had no doubt that he'd be fine. He'd come out of the cauldron whole and a full lord, any brain damage from the bullet wiped away, his eyes restored, his body unscarred.

Ten days in the cauldron, a week of recovery, and he'd be back at work as a husband, father, leader, protector of the Elf Nation.

Caddy sobbed in terror for what might have been and in gratitude for how it had turned out.

As her sobs gradually faded away – because no matter how deep the grief, crying always stops – she pulled herself together, wiped her eyes, and walked to the door.

There was already a line of people waiting to spend their time at the cauldron, talking to Kyrylo and keeping him anchored to this world. She opened the door and smiled, and thanked them. Then she left to get something to eat and comfort her children. Her family had a long ten days ahead of them.

Sarah and Caddy

Sarah sat cuddling baby Rebecca as she drifted off to sleep, and watched Ivana and Rurik play on the floor with Legos. There was a new box set of an elf village, and while they were too little to follow the elaborate instructions, they loved to play with the little people and make up their own elf homes.

She was waiting for the room to clear of visitors; Sarah wanted to talk to Caddy privately.

Caddy sat on a couch, scrolling through something on her tablet. It would have been a cosy, domestic scene if it weren't for the huge cauldron sitting in the middle of the room, steaming away.

"The elves want to put Lindy's caravan on her pyre. I don't think they should."

Caddy winced. Whenever Lindy's name came up, the guilt was overwhelming. She didn't know if she'd ever get over it.

"Why not? That's the point of the pyre, to send every bit of her back to the stars. Keeping relics of the dead is a human habit. It's creepy."

Sarah sighed and laid the sleeping baby down on the couch.

"Because she might not be dead. Or, I should say, might not have come back to this world yet. Didn't you ever wonder where I was between the time I left the Safe Haven and when I reappeared in Antarctica?"

Caddy stopped typing. "I thought you were just frozen or something. Or that it took you a long time to cross Antarctica. It's a big place."

"I was dead. I was sitting outside the Gates to the Void, chatting with the Gatekeeper. I think it was Gaia. She said it wasn't my time. That I owed too much to leave this world now. I had debts to pay."

"You died?!"

"Yep, dead as a doornail. But she (I'm pretty sure it was a she) sent me back. All I'm saying is that everyone here was sure I was dead until I wasn't. Some elves told me later they felt that I was alive well before I knocked on the research station's door, but everyone else was sure I was dead, so they kept it to themselves. They thought they were wishing too hard, fooling themselves. Maybe Lindy is dead. But maybe she's not. It would be a shame to burn up her caravan, and then she walks home and asks where it is. Why can't her pyre wait a bit?"

"She told the gods –"

Sarah didn't want to hear it, and her voice was sharp, "You don't *tell* the gods anything. They do what they want. The minute a human or a lord puts rules and restrictions on any little-G god, including the big-G one that they are all part of, we are wrong. The second we say *gods want this* or *can't do that*, we are wrong. We are setting ourselves above them. Lindy didn't *tell* them to do anything. She offered herself for the greater good. That doesn't mean they *must* take the offer."

Caddy sat back and thought about what Sarah was saying. "How long should we wait then? It's important to the elves and lords to have a fitting pyre. They'd feel they're disrespecting Lindy otherwise."

"I don't know. How long was I gone? A week? It only felt like minutes to me. That place operates in its own space and time."

The Primary looked at her tablet for a long minute and then started typing. A few people wandered in to talk to Kyrylo. The kids ran up to an elf and asked for a snack. Sarah picked up Rebecca and gave Caddy a little kiss and a hug and left to meet James.

Caddy hit send, and the email was gone.

From the Desk of Lord Cadence,

I was reminded today by Lord Sarah, quite rightly, that the gods do what the gods want to do, and it's not for us to put them in boxes, especially when it comes to our own need for ritual.

Normally, at the end of the week after a death, we would have a respectful three-day funeral pyre. In it, we return every speck of what is left of the deceased back to carbon. That is what we do.

However, Lord Sarah reminded me that we all thought she was dead, and then she reappeared on the day of her funeral. There were a few elves who sensed her back on this Earth before the rest of us knew she was alive. No one knew where she was, but those few elves felt her heartbeat, her life force.

In the very faint hope that the gods will see fit to repeat that miracle, I am going to delay Lord Aethelind's pyre for another week. I also ask every elf and lord to take a minute once a day to scan for Lord Aethelind's heartbeat. If anyone senses her, please let all of us know, and we will listen, too.

If we hear nothing, we will have given her every reasonable chance, and we'll continue with the ceremony.

Thank you for your help in this sad and stressful time.

Etc.

The Green Man

Ayu read the email, and at first he was spitting mad. Lord Cadence, the beneficiary of Lindy's sacrifice, was giving everyone false hope, a cruel and sanctimonious taunt that maybe, just maybe, Lindy could come back from death. It could only be to cover the guilt of someone else dying so her own bond-husband could live. It was so the Primary could say, *Well, I gave the gods extra time; it was their will, not mine, that Lindy stayed dead. Not my fault.*

He was the lord of life; he knew better. There was no coming back from death; there was only rebirth, and if/when Lindy was reborn, he wouldn't recognise her, and she wouldn't recognise him. The best he could hope for would be her return as a ghost, and that was worse than a clean finish and a passage through the Gates. He wouldn't wish that on her.

He had been in his flat when she exploded in the barn, and the force of the blast had imploded all of his windows and part of the wall. That night, as he sat stunned in his temporary bedroom, an elf came in with a few of his things. Some books, the poster she had given him of the Earth floating in a black sky, and, curled in a pillowcase, her long braid. She had written a note to the housekeepers. "Please deliver this to Lord Ayu. Thanks! Xx".

And then she'd walked to the barn and sacrificed herself to the gods.

He didn't cry when he found out she had died, but he cried when he pulled the silky rope out of the case. The braid held her perfume.

The Green Man read the email again. Coming back from the dead was impossible.

But so was stopping Time, and yet Lindy had done it.

"It was pretty bad when it was going on, but I survived. I always do."

Lindy was a survivor who did the impossible.

If they didn't have a pyre for her this week, he would honour her in his own way. He walked out to the terrace, sat in her chair, leaned back, shut his eyes, and listened.

If her heart was beating, he would hear it.

The Fortuneteller

This forest was damned uncomfortable. Hot, steamy, bugs everywhere, a ridiculous amount of life covered every square inch. None of it edible.

Lindy sat naked as a jaybird on a huge log, brushed the ants out of her butt crack, and contemplated her predicament. Gaia had sent her down – or maybe the gods; it didn't matter who – to this horrendous place with no clothes, no food, no nothing. Nothing but Gaia's stick, and if anything was useless, it was a stick in a jungle. The place was nothing but sticks.

She looked up. Shit, it was going to rain. And then it did. That was just the cherry on top of the hot fudge sundae.

There were monkeys; she could hear them, but couldn't see any of them. If she could see a few, she might have an idea of where she was. That might give her an idea of which direction to go to find humans and maybe some help. New World gibbons? Brazil or thereabouts. Old World apes and chimps? Africa. Orangutans? Borneo.

If she could find the monkeys, they might have information or at least point out a tree with edible fruit on it. She'd talked to a few over the years. Organ grinders often had a little sad monkey in tow, and they chattered a lot once they learned she could talk to them. The poor things were very lonely.

Maybe, she laughed to herself, I should just call Andrea. She'd bring me some food. A nice plate of pastries. Or maybe a cheese sandwich.

Well, sitting in the rain wasn't doing her any good, so she looked for shelter, and just to be silly, she called for Andrea. Nothing happened, so the elf was definitely out of range. Then she called as loud as she could for Ayu, who'd built the fucking jungle in the first place. He didn't come either.

After a few minutes of battling through the undergrowth, tripping over tree roots, and stepping into something disgusting and slimy, she found a place under some huge leaves to sit and wait for the rain to stop. It wasn't cold; it was just hard to see and walk when sheets of water were drowning a body. She sat down, and her stomach growled, so she definitely wasn't dead and dreaming.

Actually, Lindy was in a rare fine mood. She wasn't dead! She wasn't sitting on a nebula, gaping at a morphing Gatekeeper and wondering what insane avatar she'd turn into next. She was back on the Earth, somewhere, and that meant she had a chance of making it back to Aelfeham House. When she did, she'd give Ayu an earful about rainforest management.

She'd even kiss him if he came on to her again. She had been given a second chance at life, and she would take full advantage of it. Ayu was right, you have to look at the big picture and not sweat the details.

Andrea

Andrea woke up. Lord Lindy was calling her. She wanted some pączki.

For a minute, she sat in her bed and debated what to do. Was it a dream or an actual call? Asking for pączki pointed to a dream or hallucination. She didn't say "come rescue me!"

Andrea dithered, realised she was dithering, and remembered what had happened the last time she'd kept some information to herself that would have helped Lord Lindy, so the elf picked up her phone and sent an email directly to the Primary herself.

Then she tried to get back to sleep, but it was hard. She couldn't stop listening. She also couldn't stop wondering if she'd be fired tomorrow for bothering the Primary about her silly dreams at such a horrible time.

The Green Man

It was a great dream. There was Lindy, naked, covered with mud, climbing through a forest (a pretty nice one, too), bitching about not finding food, and yelling at him about it. By all the stars, she was sexy, which made it such a great dream. She was grumbling, but it was a happy grumble. Ayu could see her smile to herself when she let go with an especially creative and florid curse flow. She'd never said a single undignified word in their evening conversations, but he found that Lindy could curse like a Singapore whore, and in a wide variety of languages, too.

It made him laugh to hear such dirty words come out of that sweet mouth. That was even sexier.

She was hungry, and she couldn't find any food, yet there was food all around her. She was a temperate-zone woman and didn't know the equatorial plants. Ayu tried to point out some roots, and that woke him up, and he lost her again.

He found himself on the terrace, in her chair, a beer in one hand, and a massive hard-on in his trousers.

It wasn't the erection that bothered him; that was to be expected. It was his own heart beating so fast that he couldn't hear, which really had him discomfited. He took deep breaths, calmed himself and his heart down, and listened.

Her heart beat strong. She was alive.

For the second time in two days, he cried like a baby; this time, they were tears of joy.

Lindy

Lindy sat on another big log (they were all over the place – the rainforest was log heaven) in a pool of sunlight and let the rain dry off of her. She was looking for a tree that would be easy to climb. Even better, it would be easy to come down from, as well. She didn't want to take the express route to the forest floor with the hard stop at the end.

If she could get up high, maybe she could see something. Her problem was what to do with the useless magic stick Gaia gave her if she went climbing. It was in the way. No clothes meant no pockets. She couldn't thread it in her hair; she was practically bald from the short haircut the elf hairdresser had given her when she cut off her braid. If she laid the stupid thing down, it would surely get mixed in with the multitude of other sticks lying on the ground, and she'd lose it.

What was magic about it? She tapped it on the log and said, "Alakazam! Bring me a KFC Family meal!" Nothing happened.

Maybe that was too specific.

"Hocus Pocus, time to focus! I want roast chicken."

Nothing.

"Okay, an apple would be nice."

And in her lap fell something. It wasn't an apple. It was a mango. She looked up and saw a long-armed monkey, black with golden cheeks. He was hanging by one arm, staring at her.

"Thank you!" And she waved.

"You're welcome," he replied and swung off into the canopy.

The mango was perfect, ripe and juicy, and she ate every last bit of it, trying to remember all the while where she had seen that monkey before, and suddenly it came to her. On TV, a show about them. Rare, endangered species, hard to breed in captivity. Probably, Lindy thought, if I were in captivity, I wouldn't feel particularly sexy either.

Actually, for most of her life, she would have probably been classified as an endangered species that was hard to breed.

They were golden-cheeked gibbons, but she couldn't remember where they were from. Not Africa, she was sure. Well, that narrowed down the jungle to Asia or South America. She kept walking, looking for a good tree to climb and hoping she wasn't going in circles.

General Jameson

By the next morning, Caddy had fifteen emails in her inbox claiming to have heard Lord Aethelind's spirit and that she was alive. Most simply said they'd felt her, although an odd one, from her PA and bodyguard Warrior Elf said she was hungry and wanted some Polish pastries.

Normally, Lord James would then be tasked with finding her, but the border was now getting to a critical stage, Kyrylo was out of action for at least another week, probably two weeks, and James was carrying his load. General Jameson in Canada was given the job.

Jameson studied the assignment brief with a sense of wonder. He had been working with lords for years now, ever since he was hired away from the US Secret Service to work as a security manager on Lord Cadence's very first trip to New York. It was a big leap for him at the time, and he and his wife spent hours and hours debating before even sending in the application. She'd said go for it, so he did, even though the EN was a new entity, and he had no idea what he was really applying for. Sharona always had good instincts.

He wanted to leave the Service, but not because he disliked the job – he loved the job. His problem was his boss. Meechum was in his first term, and the autocratic, even fascist, tendencies were becoming very evident. Like a lot of old-school Secret Service agents, Jameson was LDS and pretty rigid when it came to loyalty, and he was loyal to the Constitution but not necessarily to the man who just happened to be President at the time. Jameson would take a bullet for the Constitution, but taking a bullet for a man who actively worked against it? Not so much. His wife and kids didn't deserve that.

At the time, he didn't know much about lords and elves, but he and his family certainly didn't have any problems with them, and he'd have to admit when he sent in his resume to the EN website that they all thought of the tribe as cuddly Santa's helpers. The EN paid well, very well, but what was most attractive on their website was their commitment to Balance, to equality for all, to the principles of the Constitution, even if they weren't Americans themselves.

He submitted his resume to four private security firms, major international companies – two with rather shady reputations – and was called back for interviews with all of them.

The EN's offer won hands down. After moving to Ukraine with his family, Jameson managed the security for his first elf raising, and that was the end of any doubt. He was bonded to his new job as firmly as he was bonded to his wife and family, and he loved them all dearly.

Santa's helpers were a gift from God to humanity; Jameson firmly believed that. Every new lord who made their way to Aelfeham House, every change and adaptation of his Church, every new and disappointing shift in US policy towards the EN, and the world simply made him more sure he was now working on the side of the angels.

Now he was the senior military leader for the EN in North America, and he and his family were very happy living in Ottawa. Ukraine was an adventure for his girls, but Ottawa was a lovely town, and they spoke English, which was better for Sharona, who was lonely in rural Ukraine.

He had vast resources at his disposal, including millions of elves in Europe and Canada, and he could call on any of them for help. His human soldiers, operatives, and employees broke twenty thousand. The Canadian government would jump through hoops to help him find a lord.

Now he was tasked with finding a lost lord who had died and been to the gates of Heaven or Hell or the Spirit World or wherever, and had now returned to the world and was lost. There were elves who said they could feel her life force – her heartbeat – and James had long ago learned not to ignore elves.

The Little People were hard to figure out sometimes, and their tendency to be rigidly literal could be frustrating, but never discounted. It was his job to interpret what they said, not dismiss it because it didn't conform to his way of thinking.

This lord, they said, was of immense power, but her power wasn't really useful for day-to-day survival. She could stop time, but she couldn't start a fire with it or fly or feed herself. James knew all that. He had managed Lord Lindy's extraction, and while he hadn't known about the time ability when he met her, he was impressed by her practical survival skills. She was adaptable and smart.

He ported home for lunch and told his wife a lord was lost and he'd be working double time until he found her. He didn't have to go home, but he always told her these things personally because if something ever happened to him, he didn't want their last encounter to be on the phone. Sharona was interested and optimistic. "Ted, you've guided lords home before. I'm sure this will work out."

"I've met this one already; it's Lord Aethelind. I just didn't know at the time I was meeting an angel! She died and came back from the Spirit World!" An angel! Sharona had to think about that for a minute.

They were sitting in the kitchen, and their housekeeper elf brought the general a sweet cider and a sandwich, and the worry on his face was palpable. The elf didn't leave when he set the plate down like he usually did, but stood to the side, wringing his hands, and his eyes never left the General.

Jameson looked at the elf and smiled. The elves took very good care of his family, and the Warrior Elves did a great job guarding them. "What's wrong, Jim? You want to say something."

The elf looked up, beseeching. "You have to find Lord Aethelind, Gen Jameson. You just have to. She's not just another lord. Lord Ayu is bonding with her. We can tell. If she dies again, she won't come back. How many times will the gods send someone back? If we lose her, we'll lose Lord Ayu, and that would be a disaster. If we don't die from the orcs, we'll die when the world dies."

The General put his sandwich down. Who was Lord Ayu, and why did his death mean the world would die? He didn't know that Lord Aethelind was bonded. That wasn't in his background report.

So he spent the next hour quizzing Jim on all the things that every elf knew and just assumed the humans knew, too.

Lord Ayu, Jim said, was Lord Ayu. It took Jameson a good five minutes of careful questioning just to get past that one.

Lord Ayu was The Green Man, the personification of the entire world's life force. A man who was made along with the Earth the day it coalesced from random atoms and was born. For uncounted millennia, he just was, not sentient and yet not dead. Just there. And as the Earth matured, so did he.

A little bit of self-awareness, a little bit of boredom, a little bit of shoving a pebble here and there as the Earth cooled and solidified, a little bit of stirring of the chemical soups that formed in rock pools just to see the pretty swirls, and he accidentally created the first slime mould. There was a lot of joy when something wonderful like that happened.

Lord Ayu had a brother, Lord Neptune, and they talked to each other, and that kept both from going insane with loneliness. Their natural brotherly rivalry kept them apart enough to develop their own interests and together enough to encourage and love each other. Neptune took the role of the younger brother, the follower, and went to the seas when they formed. Three and a half billion years ago, Ayu had made a tiny, single prokaryotic organism as a joke and snuck it into Neptune's barren, dead sea, and from that single cell, life evolved.

Ayu wasn't a god; he was (surely) made by the gods when they made the world, so while human religions taught that god/s created Earthly life, that wasn't quite true – except indirectly. The gods created the creator of life. Ayu evolved into a lord, and lords were tools of the gods just like elves, orcs, and humans.

Time passed. Ayu and Neptune learned and grew, and developed their own realms and their own personalities. Their huge ages didn't weigh on them; both were pretty here-and-now creatures, and the long, long boring sections of their lives simply condensed in their minds as "then". They slept a lot, but as they slept, the simple organisms Ayu had made as a joke to amuse Neptune evolved.

Neither bonded because, in the beginning, there was no mate to bond to. And later, as humans, elves and more lords evolved from that first single protozoa, the two primordial lords simply weren't tempted. Neptune never found a lord because lords didn't live in his water world, and the merfolk were sea elves, not immortal lords, just long-lived. Caddy was the only lord he'd ever found who smelled right, and he screwed that one up.

Ayu found Gaia, but she turned out to be a disaster. Maybe on some deep level, he'd known from the beginning she wasn't the right person for him. He didn't bond, and his soul remained whole and unshared.

It took Jameson the rest of the hour to tease out exactly why the death of this one lord, however ancient, would affect the world. Lords did die; that was proven in history. Lords Lena and Lester both died. Lester from a bullet to the brain, Lena from bond sickness.

Lords died, and the world moved on.

Jim wasn't a farmer, and he wasn't a particularly deep thinker. He was a housekeeper, an elf of many talents, but his lord management classes were pretty basic. You feed the creatures, you make them comfortable so they don't roam too far, you find them mates so they bonk like bunnies and make the pheromones that their elf tribe depended on for their own existence. If an elf clan was lucky with their lord, they also got protection from orcs and humans. That was pretty much Jim's level of understanding. Successful elf clans were consummate ranchers of lords, whether the lords realised it or not.

But he tried his best to explain to the General that Lord Ayu was different. As the instigator of life, if he died, life would stop evolving on Earth. It would simply stop adapting to new problems, and now there were a lot of problems, mostly human-created.

When things went to shit, Ayu would tweak and push and nudge, and an extinct species would be replaced by something else, the way the dinosaurs were replaced after the meteor killed them off. If there had been no Lord Ayu, nothing would have happened after the meteor hit. No natural selection, no evolution, no humans, no nothing. Eventually, like the other dead planets, Earth would have died from continual assaults from meteors, solar wind blasts, and its own internal combustion. Neptune's fish would have eventually died off, and then he would have died of starvation or gone back into a formless, dreamless sleep. Neptune wasn't a creator of life. He didn't have Ayu's talent that way.

Lord Ayu could sleep for millennia and let the world go on autopilot, but when he woke, he looked around, saw where things were out of balance, put his thumb on the proverbial scales, and rebalanced life. When he was awake, each tweak was so subtle no one noticed. But now he was back awake, and the elves expected some major shifts. They saw him watching and thinking. Soon – and Jim shivered. Life would get interesting.

But not if he was bond-sick. Not if he died. If Lord Ayu died, the Earth would die with him and become just another rocky planet around a minor star.

When he was done, a grim-faced Jameson left his cosy home and his shell-shocked wife contemplating ecological armageddon, called an aide, and they both ported to Aelfeham House to talk to this Lord Ayu, a lord so powerful that he held the fate of the world in his hands.

General Jameson and Lord Ayu

The poster hung on his wall now in a simple wood frame. She had laughed and said she had given him the world, and while Ayu got the joke, he was also aware, whether she meant it that way or not, that Lindy had given him her world, and in doing so, she'd completed his.

He hadn't really understood until she died. Before she flamed out, he'd been interested in her, maybe even falling in love. No one had ever sat and talked with him like she did, not ever. He didn't need to see her, smell her, or touch her, and yet he was falling in love just talking to her. If someone had described LeeAnne's epistolary romance with Wendell, Ayu would have recognised the parallels.

Lindy liked him.

The night she gave him the poster, he touched her for the first time, and she shivered under his fingers. He couldn't stop drinking in her perfume, and she responded to him. He heard her gasp as she fell, scent drunk, and her eyes glowed, and little traces of green fire flickered on her skin. She was as sexy as hell. But unlike Gaia, who would have taken that moment to complete the attachment, Lindy ran off.

She wasn't going to bond accidentally, and she wasn't going to let him fall either. She was kinder than Gaia and smarter and more disciplined than the both of them.

It was too late, of course; he was already halfway there.

When the elf popped into his room and told him that General Jameson was waiting in the Breakfast Room and (respectfully) asked to have a meeting with Lord Ayu, he was irritated. Ayu had planned to sit and meditate and see if he could hear Lindy's heartbeat again. Maybe even dream watch her and make sure she was okay. But the elf said General Jameson was an important man and had been ordered by Lord Cadence to mount a search for Lord Aethelind, and that was enough to make Ayu go see him.

General Jameson stood up when the lord walked into the room, but Lord Ayu was the first to offer his hand.

Jameson would tell his wife later that he had never seen a lord who simply glowed. Oh, it was at a low level, but when a cloud outside darkened the room, he could see a faint, eerie, blue glow around the lord. The elves and lords were always talking about how they could feel power around the Elementals, but this was the first time he had seen it. It probably helped the glow that Lord Ayu was emotional about losing Lord Aethelind.

When Sharona asked what he looked like, her husband had to think. "If you stood next to him at the cash register in Walmart, you'd think – tallish, a guy who does hard work for a living. Not a handsome movie star like Lord Neptune, not pretty. But I think women would say he was very good-looking. I think he smiles a lot; that's how his face rests. Then there are the lord parts. Huge ears, white hair in a braid that reaches his waist. Long braided beard. Blue eyes that glow so bright you can't see them. He was wearing a Hawaiian shirt, old jeans, and slip-on canvas shoes with a hole in one toe." She laughed and laughed at the image of a demi-god in a Hawaiian shirt.

Jameson and his aide, Major Kimber, sat in the chairs by the fireplace and told the lord what they could do and what their problems were. They were prepared to go anywhere in the world, but they needed to know where. The EN had huge resources, and Jameson had personally managed the extraction of Lord Aethlind, and he respected her abilities.

"She's a survivor," said Lord Ayu. "That's what she calls herself, and she's right. I've been reading the human history that she lived through, and it's horrendous. If she stays in the forests, she will be safer, but that will make it harder for us to find her. When she contacts humans – that's when the risks start. There's nothing in the natural world that will hurt her – except humans and orcs."

Nodding, Jameson looked at Kimber and asked her if the intel elves were monitoring communications traffic for anything unusual. Kimber smiled wryly. "We're always monitoring, sir. But, yes, we've upped the tempo and changed the AI filters a bit. We won't see her with a Romani caravan this time, but just in case we're following horse sales, missing horses, that sort of thing."

"Lord Ayu, when you sense her, can you sense anything about her environment that can help us?" Jameson turned to the lord. “The elves we’re talking to just hear her heartbeat, but they don’t sense anything else. One elf who knew her, her PA in Warsaw, said she was hungry. I mean, if we just knew if she was cold or hot or roaming a steppe or desert – that would eliminate huge swaths of the Earth, and we could focus on the possible places.”

“Oh! Yes, I can tell you she’s in a jungle. I heard her bitch at me about how there wasn’t enough to eat in a jungle, and I wanted to tell her what to do; there is, really – but I woke up and lost her.” He looked frustrated. “I guess I shouldn’t complain that I had any vision of her at all, but these dreams are like I’m watching a TV screen when I see her. I can’t talk back, or that would solve a lot of problems.”

Kimber was typing as fast as she could, and then looked up. “Sir, could you try to dream of her again and next time, instead of concentrating on her, concentrate on the jungle itself? Wouldn’t each jungle of the world have its own plants and animals? If you could describe a plant or a bug, or something like that, we can pinpoint her location even better. If you can’t describe a plant –” And she faded away, embarrassed. Of course, The Green Man would be able to describe a plant.

Ayu just grinned at her, not offended at all. It was an excellent suggestion. He could probably pinpoint her location down to ten square miles if he saw the right combination of plants and bugs, and he told them so.

With that, General Jameson thanked Ayu and got up. “We all have work to do. Lord Ayu, please send me an email or text at any time, day or night, if something occurs to you or you sense her. Someone is always monitoring my communications, and we’re a 24/7 operation. We will contact you the second we find out anything. If we can pinpoint her – *when* we pinpoint her – we’ll talk about the next stages. We don’t have any elves or porting stations in parts of the world with jungles, so this will be a human-style operation. But you'll be there every step of the way."

The general and his aide left, and Ayu went to the buffet and began to load up. He always dreamt better on a full stomach, and after he had lunch, he planned to "Sleep and perchance to dream".

Lord James Cowen

When Kyrylo died, James was in his office chairing the morning SITREP briefing and managing a perfectly normal day in his perfectly abnormal life. He, like all the other lords, was immediately sledgehammered into the hole that once was Kyrylo, and when he sprang up out of his chair, his eyes glowing in horror and his body flaming, his human staff didn't know what to do. Then the elves started screaming, and all hell broke loose.

A minute later (was it as long as that?) Kyrylo wasn't dead, but Lord Aethelind, who he had never met, was.

Five minutes later, he was told that Lord Kryrylo was being ported to a cauldron, that he was in a bad way. Shot by a sniper while inspecting the Wall.

Six minutes later, James was in charge of the whole fucking EN army until further notice.

The EN military leadership was well-drilled for emergencies; they had regularly practised for the Primaries' kidnapping, incapacitation, or death. James knew what to do, but theory and practice are never the same, are they? You can dress rehearse until you're blue in the face, but opening night is still terrifying.

He didn't sleep for two days until his aide Charlotte and his wife Sarah put their formidable feet down. He wasn't going to do anyone any good if he fell apart, and they were right, of course. Women always were over that sort of thing. He was told to sleep for six hours, and if he didn't eat a good meal, Sarah was going to port him to a desert island until he did.

But by then, they knew Kryrylo was going to live, and Lord Aethelind's pyre was being prepared even though there was nothing left to burn. James was too busy to think too much about that; his only focus was on protecting the living, not worrying about the niceties for the dead. But at odd moments, he had flashbacks to when Sarah had died and that week of mind-numbing despair he'd suffered. He had bonded to her before he knew what bonding was, and her death would have eventually killed him, but … but … but …

Too many "buts" and "what ifs" and "could have beens" to think about, every one of them awful.

The Russians were ecstatic that one of their snipers had popped off a lucky, one-in-a-billion shot and killed the Primary Warlord, Kyrylo. Soloyev, their general, knew almost immediately. The reaction of the elves and lords to Kyrylo's death was not hidden from their thousands of EN employees, and in that number, there were spies and turncoats. There always were, and they only needed one to send a message to Russia that the EN had been decapitated.

Soloyev immediately told his people to prepare for an assault. A real one, to test the defences of the EN and their new, post-NATO, post-US European Alliance. He positioned three armies of orcs at different points on the Wall to split the EN/EA forces. They didn't know which one would be the flashpoint; no one did but Soloyev, but they were ready.

For years, this moment was what they had been preparing for. A new Russian invasion was exactly what the US kept saying would never happen, and yet, here they were, days away from one. Just where they didn't know.

James wondered what Zelensky had been thinking two days before the Russians invaded in '22, when everyone had been saying it would never happen, even though intel reports showed Russian forces massing on the border. Had he been thinking of anything? Or had the former Ukrainian president been running on adrenaline, bad coffee, and prayers? He would have to ask him the next time he saw him in Brussels.

What did Zelensky do with his wife and kids? James' wife was a lord herself, a Warrior Lord Elemental of immense value to the EN, his oldest son a lord Ranger, his daughter a lord trainee Ranger, and his youngest son a drone operator. Every lord over the age of thirteen had a military job or civic responsibility. That's what species survival required; that's what genocide mandated. Then there was their baby, Rebecca, who depended on all of them.

James wouldn't let himself think about his children as he barked out orders and positioned his assets. Soloyev certainly wouldn't.

Lindy

The black gibbon came back, this time with his family. Primates are curious creatures; the gibbon's name was Archibald, and his lovely, golden wife's name was Xi. They had three children, each two years apart, and they all wanted to see this lord who they recognised as not human and who could talk to them.

Lindy had a nice conversation with Archibald and Xi. They told her where the mango tree was and shared the location of a few other fruits, but they spoke so fast that Lindy didn't catch it all. No, they didn't know of any other humans in their territory, but then they avoided them. They didn't like to live in built-up human areas – too noisy – and humans had a bad habit of clearing out the trees so the gibbons couldn't swing between them easily. But if Lindy followed the morning sun, she'd eventually get to a plantation where humans worked. They didn't know where the workers lived.

Xi cautioned Lindy about the dangers of going into the human range; the humans had guns and traps. Lindy told her not to worry; she understood the dangers.

In the meantime, she followed the gibbons to the mango tree, and when she found it, she gorged.

The Green Man

Ayu heard her as if she were in the next room. "I like your mangos, Ayu! I ate a lot of them. I hope they don't give me the shits!" That made him laugh, and laughing woke him up. But for the briefest of minutes, he had a good look at her and where she was. She was still naked, and her face was covered in sticky mango juice like a greedy child's. There was a yellow monkey sitting near her, eating a mango, too.

He called an elf for help, and together they looked up yellow monkeys on his tablet (one day he would meet this Google fellow and thank him) and found, after a lot of scrolling, a photo of what he'd seen. The female yellow-cheeked gibbon. Humans, it seemed, liked to look at photos of the males of a species when they illustrated an article, so he scrolled past the gibbon pages because the males pictured were black. After a bit of work, he found the right one, and as soon as he did, he sent Gen Jameson a text.

"Wild mango tree. Yellow-cheeked gibbon."

He went to take a shower and change his clothes before he went to the Breakfast Room to see what was left on the buffet, but before he left the flat, he already had a reply. It was a map of all of the areas that had both mangos (which were common) and golden-cheeked gibbons (which were not common). It was sad to see how small their range was, and Ayu decided to do something about that to thank them for taking care of Lindy.

Cambodia, Laos, and Vietnam. Mostly Cambodia.

They were narrowing it down.

Caddy and Kyrylo

Right on time, according to Mandy's chart, which considered the War Lord's weight and degree of damage, Kyrylo's egg floated to the top of the goo, and everyone breathed a sigh of relief and celebrated. Caddy looked into the huge pot, and what she could see in the semi-transparent sac looked perfectly normal. She saw the faint outlines of two arms, two legs, the curve of his spine – it all looked just as it should, with no weird animal parts that would give any indication he was going to emerge as a satyr or something like that. She couldn't tell if his scars were gone, but she could only assume they were, just like hers had disappeared when she was re-born.

She had to go off by herself for half an hour and have a good cry. In the years since she emerged from her own cauldron, she'd never thought of what he'd gone through while she was floating in there. A couple of people at the time had said that Kyrylo had taken it hard, but in the happiness of recovery, their words hadn't sunk in. Now, with her own experience, it did, and her new recognition of his steadfast love simply made her cherish him all the more. He had suffered as she re-formed and had nursed her back to health twice, both times with no prior experience that would help give him hope she would emerge healthy. Now it was her turn.

As soon as he floated to the surface, Caddy brought Ivana and Rurik in and held them up to the rim and let them have a look.

"See! Daddy's sleeping! He'll be awake soon! He was sick, but soon he'll be much better!" They weren't too sure about the cauldron, but "daddy sleeping and will wake up soon" was a concept they could understand, and they were happy with that.

The only problem Caddy had with the kids was that the nanny elves had to watch Ivana like a hawk. She kept running up to the cauldron and trying to throw toys in and yelling, "Wakey, wakey!"

The man was obviously oversleeping, and she had plans. On a day when Ivana was particularly trying and Rurik drew a picture of Kyrylo on the side of the cauldron (it was very good and really funny, and Caddy told the elves to take a photo of it for Kyrylo to see later), Caddy had to ban them from the room for a day.

On the very day marked on the calendar, almost to the anticipated hour, the ever-punctual Kyrylo exploded from the cauldron. Caddy was a high-strung bundle of nervous energy as she waited in the hall with her family and friends and watched the elves running around like dervishes. She grabbed one unfortunate soul as he ran by, and her fierce eyes almost unmanned him, but all she wanted to know was "Is he all right?" The nurse elf grinned and gave her a thumbs up. "Yes, Lord Cadence, he's 99.998 per cent as he should be." Then the man dashed off.

Stunned, Caddy looked at the back of the disappearing elf. Ninety-nine point nine nine eight per cent? What the hell did that mean?

All she could do was take a deep breath and put on her calm face for the people gathered in the hall. Whatever mistake or flaw Kyrylo suffered in the cauldron, they'd work through it. She hoped he didn't have an extra eye. Everyone kept saying they hoped he came back with all of his eyes, and "all" was a very vague term.

When the elf came to fetch her for her first look at her bond-husband, Caddy walked through the door – and there lay Kyrylo, bald, puffy, and perfect. Without a beard and head hair, he looked a lot like he did when they first met, when he was totally clean-shaven.

He was asleep, as all the newly re-born were, and lying on a pristine bed, a blanket covering most of his body. But from what Caddy could see, Kyrylo had been reborn as he was meant to be. For the first time, both sides of his face matched, with (two!) closed eyes, no scars, no puckers and divots from missing muscle, no damage down the left side of his body. The ancient scars from his encounter with the IED that had almost killed him were gone. He had his left pinky finger. The new damage from the sniper was gone.

She shut her own eyes; it was too much to see him, and she gave out a big, shuddering breath. Then she sat down in the chair to wait for him to wake up and spent the next hour staring at him and thanking the gods for their kindness.

Recovery from reforming and re-birthing usually took about ten days, but Kyrylo was, as always, determined and efficient.

By the next day, he was trying to talk to her between the frequent meals and naps, and he was obviously delighted with binocular vision. Since he had two eyes for the first twenty-eight years of his life, his brain immediately re-adapted, and his vision was fine if a bit near-sighted. He had full elf ears, and his blue eyes were an intense, bright sky-blue with no flecks of grey and sharp black rims around the irises. Like Caddy, the effect was startling to humans. He had animal eyes. Lord eyes.

By day four, he was insisting on getting staff reports and was checking his email even when Caddy yelled at him and told him to slow down. Kyrylo would just smile, nod, and the minute she left the room, he was back at work, ordering Bram to do this or that and sneaking Lord James in for quick consultations.

On day seven, the nurse who made sure the War Lord wouldn't be improperly touched during his recovery stopped shadowing him, and Caddy did her own sneaking into his office. She had her first kiss and snuggled with him while he tried to nap on his big office sofa, the same sofa where she'd jumped on him when she'd been impatient with her own recovery.

Kyrylo was too disciplined to do anything more than a kiss without clearance from Dr Mandy, but he did kiss her back. Then he said he had a secret he wanted her to know, something for her to think about before they shared a bed again. She tensed up. Here was the .002 per cent thing again. Impotence?

He whispered in her ear. "Jack once told me that when he went into the cauldron, he visualised himself a couple of inches taller. When he came out, he was. While I was in the cauldron, I woke up a couple of times and visualised myself with my kink. I'm pretty familiar with that body part. I knew exactly what it should look like." He smiled, his blue eyes snapping, then he fell back asleep, still smiling.

All was right in the Melnyk household, and a few days later, Kyrylo was back at work, and the entire cauldron incident was just a bad memory. And as far as Caddy was concerned, her bond-husband was one hundred per cent perfect.

Lindy

Walking through the jungle was slow going. Occasionally, she'd find an animal trail, but if she wanted to stick to an eastern course, they were few and far between. She had to make sure she wasn't going in circles, something that could happen in any forest and was just a waste of time and energy. If she used her magic to move stuff out of the way, that also used up more calories, and she was getting sick of mangos.

Lindy could hear animals. Wild dogs, something like a jackal, yipped around her. There were a few large cats. She even heard some elephants, but they were far away. It would have been nice to run across one and see if it would let her ride it, but that didn't happen. There were lots of deer and wild pigs. She wasn't worried about the animals; they were more afraid of her, not knowing exactly what she was, and their fear was probably why she just heard them from afar but didn't see them. Other than the gibbon family, who were now long gone, the wildlife avoided her.

But what was really a pain in the ass was the pain in the ass she got from being naked. It wasn't cold, but clothes protected against stinging insects, branches, thorns, and other nasties. Shoes! She really missed shoes. Every time she stepped in some variety of poop, she missed shoes.

She wondered what she would do when she ran into civilisation. Lindy could just imagine the reception she'd get when the locals saw a filthy, naked fairy wandering into a village and waving a magic chopstick. There was no hiding her ears. They'd either build a shrine to her or kill her and eat her. But she'd cross that bridge when she came to it.

While she was getting tired of her Jungle Jane adventure, she was still in a good mood. She was alive, the big picture was good, and a bit of poop squishing between her toes was the least of her worries.

At night, she'd climb into the low branches of a tree and look for a place to rest. The first time she tried to make a little nest like the forest gorillas and chimps she'd seen in the nature documentaries, Lindy almost fell out of the tree and gave up on that pretty quickly. She didn't have the knack, and it was more trouble than it was worth.

One night, while she was sitting high in a tree and trying not to fall off her branch, she half-dozed, and in her dream she saw Ayu. He was at the buffet in the Breakfast Room, loading up his plate. He looked good – healthy and handsome – and he turned to Rita and said, "Yeah, we're still looking for her, and we're closer –" And he plopped a big chunk of meatloaf right in the middle of his mashed potatoes. Lindy could have moaned. The food! She was so taken by the food she didn't think about what he'd said until much later.

It was a dream, of course, but it would certainly be nice if Ayu were looking for her. But how would he even know she was alive? Lindy thought about DreamRita standing there, talking to him. She was always on the hunt, and while she was a loyal friend, if Lindy weren't around, Rita wouldn't think twice about setting her Elf Nation bluecoat cap on Ayu.

The next morning, Lindy woke up with more determination than ever to find civilisation, bum a phone call to the nearest friendly embassy, and tell the EN to get their collective asses down to whatever forgotten part of the world she was in and rescue her. She needed to get home before some other horny female lord decided to go sit on the terrace in the dark and talk to The Green Man.

As she walked through the unchanging jungle, she yelled at Ayu. "Ayu! Braid your beard! You're looking a bit shaggy. I'm on my way!" And she set off.

Ayu

Ayu sat straight up in bed. Lindy had told him to braid his beard; he was looking shaggy, and she was on her way. That was good, and yes, he did need to comb out his beard and rebraid it, so she must have seen him in her own dream. But the best part was that when she disappeared into the jungle, he saw the dogs shadowing her. They wouldn't bother her; they were simply curious. They knew instinctively that any threat they made to this creature was dangerous, but they couldn't resist getting as close as they could and having a sniff. That's what dogs did, even wild dogs.

He went to Mr Google and, just like the elf taught him, started searching for pictures of wild dogs. The pack in his dreams wasn't a feral domesticated pack; it was wild, its own species.

It was a dhole, and there were only a couple of places in the world where the range of dholes and yellow-cheeked gibbons overlapped. Cambodia. And only a couple of places in Cambodia, at that.

Ayu could have danced, but before he did, he sent a text to General Jameson. "I saw a dhole. Cambodia?"

Then he went to the bathroom to take a good shower and rebraid his beard. It needed it.

General Jameson

Jameson talked to his elves in intel, and they supported Lord Ayu's guess, although he had a suspicion that if Lord Ayu told them to look in the strip clubs of downtown Alpha Centauri, they'd support that, too.

But he had an extraction team on standby, and he sent a text back to Lord Ayu asking him to please have the elves transport him to Ottawa, where they would have a briefing with the team. Then they would port across to Lethbridge, which would save about five hours of flight time, and from there fly to Phnom Penh. Vancouver to Phnom Penh was eighteen hours.

When things settled down, he was going to ask if they could set up some transfer nodes in some of the more out-of-the-way places. Eighteen hours of flight time! It was like going back to 2025!

Lindy

In any other country, the road would be considered a red muddy trail; in Cambodia, it was Highway 76. Lindy sat hidden in the tall grass that lined both sides of the road just to watch for a while. She didn't know the road was Highway 76 or even that she was in Cambodia; all she knew was that the road she could see went from north to south. It was two lanes wide, but from the car tracks in the mud, everyone drove straight down the middle because why the hell not?

Before the big War to End All Wars (a lie), she'd guided her caravan down many roads like this in Austria-Hungary, Romania, Poland, and Germany. She'd even wandered down to the disintegrating Ottoman Empire in the winter. These roads were mud pits and wheel-eaters. They were roads that looked perfectly reasonable, but given a bit of rain, the unwary would splash through what looked to be a shallow puddle and find themselves knee-deep in gluey mud and spend the next three days replacing a broken axle.

It was roads like this that made her buy five heavy horses when she was flush with money from selling her house. Intellectually, she knew that five was overkill, and two or three was more than enough, but if her life was at stake, she would spend the money. In the end, she'd never needed all those horses, and she'd found that she didn't need the money either.

As she watched, the traffic looked fairly regular – trucks, lots of little scooters and motorcycles, an occasional car. Most were rickety old junkers, but not all. She couldn't read the licence plates as they whizzed by because she couldn't see them from where she was hiding in the grass. The question now was which way was closest to a village or town? North or south?

She tapped Gaia's magic chopstick on the palm of her hand and then decided to find a mango tree or some other wild fruit and have some lunch. Where there was a road, there would be houses, and soon she'd be around humans. She needed to be well fed enough to use her magic, just in case.

During her midday mango, she decided to parallel the road going south, about a hundred or more yards to the east. Just close enough to keep track of the road, but not close enough to be seen herself. She didn't want to be noticed, not because she cared about being naked – she was past any embarrassment or modesty now – but because she didn't want anyone to shoot her for being a witch. And she certainly didn't want to attract orcs. Lindy was sure she stank like a friggin' cesspit.

The Green Man

When he told the housekeeper elf that he was leaving in the morning for Ottawa, the woman nodded and said she'd pack a bag for him, but was there anything in particular he wanted her to pack? Ayu thought for a minute and really couldn't think of anything. He'd arrived naked in Lowestoft, and other than some colourful Hawaiian shirts he liked (they were a lot more comfortable than the blue wool uniform), he'd just wear whatever she wanted to pack up. He was planning on coming back.

With Lindy, if all went well.

Then he called the elf back and asked her to pack some things for Lord Aethelind, too. The poor woman was running around the Cambodian jungle naked and would probably like something to throw on. Humans seemed to have a thing about being clothed, and he didn't want her to feel underdressed on the journey back.

Ottawa was fine. The minute Aya stepped into the Ottawa transport node, two RumLot Security captains walked up and introduced themselves as his escorts and aides for the day. Surprised they knew who he was, he grinned; it was the braided beard, wasn't it? No, they said, it was the epaulettes on his lord's bluecoat. Only three people had the full moon, and he wasn't a woman, and he didn't have an eyepatch, so he must be Lord Ayu. He didn't know that only Caddy and Kyrylo had full moons. He'd never noticed.

The briefing was pretty short.

They had permission from the Cambodian government to come in as a private entity to look for a lost EN citizen. That permission had cost the EN quite a bit of money, and everyone needed to be aware of the risks of working in a very poor country with high levels of public corruption.

There were public aspects of the mission, mostly to provide noise and cover for the stealthier operatives.

The intel people were combing the area for any mention of a lord, fairy, whatever, but nothing had turned up yet. When some bit of good intel does show up, they'll set up working groups to go out and comb the area. Some agents will be disguised as Western tourists, and there are operatives already in Phnom Penh.

Lord Ayu would be scanning for Lord Aethelind constantly, and if he decided to go off hunting for her, they would provide whatever assistance he required.

At this point, it was a very fluid mission, and everyone needed to be on their toes and open to any eventuality. They were pretty sure Lord Aethelind was in Cambodia and would eventually be noticed or pop up on her own. They needed to be ready to get to her and recover her.

That was pretty much it. A company of soldiers and specialists were going to charge off into the unknown and hoped the needle in the haystack was where they thought it would be. If they were lucky, it wouldn't all be a wild goose chase.

Lord Ayu, The Green Man, the first man, the most powerful man on the planet, found he really, really hated flying. Despised everything about it. He hated the noise of the jets, the foul air in the cabins, and he had attacks of airsickness the entire eighteen-hour flight. The first two hours of the journey were spent lying in the master cabin trying to pop his ears and feeling miserably nauseated. The company doctor wouldn't give him anything because he was afraid of a reaction ("Look what happened to Lord Freyja!"), and airsickness wasn't a fatal disease. Ayu could have argued that point, but he was too sick.

Ayu had never been ill before, not once in four and a half billion years. He had been hungry and tired, and he'd felt pain when he did the normal, stupid things like stubbing his toe, but never sick. It was a new experience and one he fervently hoped would never be repeated.

General Jameson walked into the forward cabin, looked at the miserable man, and told him to go sit up with the pilots; he'd feel better if he could see out of the big windows up front. Ayu almost told him to go fuck off, but he would do anything to stop his stomach from trying to exit through his gullet. Jameson was right, and while the nausea didn't entirely go away, it calmed quite a bit when Ayu's brain could align what it was seeing and the motion his sensitive ears felt. Plus, once he was there, it was fascinating seeing the Earth from forty thousand feet.

Lindy and The Little Girl

The woman was taking down clothes from the line; a little girl of about ten was helping her, and running around like dervishes between the two, a pair of six-year-old boys played. They looked like twins.

This was the first house – a tin shack – Lindy had come across as she walked down the road, and she watched them from the brush, wondering how she was going to steal something to wear.

It wasn't the first time she had stolen drying clothes from an isolated house. Not even the second time. Back when she was young and her hair was still red, cloth was a precious commodity, and clothes meant you were part of the Christian God's kingdom.

Animals went naked, and naked people were treated like animals. Slaves and serfs went naked or lived in literal rags, and it wasn't even worth commenting on to drive down a rutted road and pass naked beggars and pilgrims.

Cloth was worth its weight in gold, sometimes literally. Every thread had to be hand-spun. Every inch of fabric was hand-woven on a loom, and looms weren't something a person could haul in a caravan. Before mechanical looms, a poor woman might have one fourth-hand dress she would wear for years. Decades.

Lindy saw many naked, starving people barely surviving on the fringes of society as she'd wandered around Eastern Europe, and it was cold there! Not like here. She felt bad taking clothes from people who were obviously poor, but needs must, as they said in Suffolk. She would ask the elves to send the family something to pay them back; she was sure they would do that for her.

So Lindy watched the woman fold the laundry and debated the best way to swipe one of the skirts and a t-shirt the villager was carefully taking down. The skirts were some sort of wrap, and Lindy knew the squares of cloth were wrap skirts because the woman was wearing one. The t-shirts and tank tops were average, modern wear.

Then one of the boys fell, skinned his knee, and screamed like it was being amputated without anaesthesia, and the woman, surely his mother, picked him up and took him inside the shack.

The girl stayed outside to finish taking down the rest of the clothes, and the other boy followed his mother inside. Watching major surgery on his brother was much more interesting than watching his sister fold underpants.

Lindy mentally unpegged a skirt, and it flew up and over the line and over to the bush where she was hiding; the girl froze and watched open-mouthed as she watched the skirt fly off by itself. Then Lindy took one of the tank tops. It unpegged itself and followed the skirt. It only took a minute to dress, and with the wrap skirt on, she was able to put Gaia's Magic-but-Useless Chopstick in the waistband so she didn't have to carry it in her hand all the time. That was a blessing, right there.

A rustle in the grass, and Lindy looked up. The girl was standing in front of her, her eyes as big as dinner plates and her mouth a little o of astonishment. Lindy smiled and put her finger to her mouth in the universal "don't talk" sign and then said in Elvish, "I'm sorry to steal your mother's clothes, but I need them now. I'll pay her back."

The girl slapped her hands over her mouth and jumped up and down in giggling, wiggling ecstasy. Then she put her hands together in a *sampeah* and whispered, the loud way children do, "Mrenh kongveal! You are welcome!" Then she pleaded with the mrenh kongveal Good Luck Fairy, "Can I touch you?"

Lindy smiled and shrugged and reached out her hand, and pointed a finger, and the girl did the same, and they touched fingertips. The girl squealed with delight and turned and ran back to the house, forgetting all about being quiet and screaming to her mother. "Mrenh kongveal, mrenh kongveal!" But when she spun around to have one last look, the fairy was gone.

The Mrenh Kongveal Good Luck Fairy

In half an hour, the village was abuzz. Little Channery from the last house had seen a mrenh kongveal! The fairy had stolen some clothes, but she had promised to pay back Botum, her mother. A few people were a bit jealous, but the family was a nice one, and if anyone could use the luck, they could.

But what really got the village talking was that a mrenh kongveal was spotted at all. The little girl's glimpse of the magic people was a very good omen for everyone. When the elves reappeared in Europe, the wise people of the village said it was only a matter of time before they came back to Cambodia. When they did, even the poorest would have some good luck, and there it was, physical proof that they were right. The poorest house in the village was the first to spot one of the luckiest of creatures, and now everyone would keep their eyes open wide. That night, almost every house dragged out its old-fashioned spirit houses (to a Westerner, they looked like bird houses) and put out an offering, just in case.

An hour after the first villager called his mother to gossip about the mrenh kongveal the AI filters in Ukraine recorded the call, and then a flood of calls. General Jameson was still three hours away from landing when he received the message.

A credible report that a "fairy" was spotted not far from the target area. She (a female) had stolen some clothes.

Jameson immediately told Lord Ayu and then the soldiers and staff. A shock of electricity crackled through the plane. No one was sleepy or jet-lagged now. They had a lead.

Lord Aethelind, Jungle Queen of the Mrenh Kongveal

She was in Cambodia.

Lindy squatted in the tall grass at the very edge of the village and watched the villagers do their normal everyday life thing. Barefoot children played in the dirt street, skinny dogs sprawled in the shade, and old men and women sat in doorways and watched over everyone else's business. Other than the few cars, scooters, and bicycles, the scene could have been anywhere in the world, any time back to the Middle Ages.

She figured out she was in Cambodia from the signs on the sides of the delivery trucks. She could read the language if she put her mind and magic to it, and one said "Cambodia's Finest Laundry Detergent". That was all she needed. The signs on the shop fronts were still a bit too far and hidden to make out, but she could see a few letters here and there in the curly Cambodian script.

The little girl wasn't afraid of her. Cambodia, from what she remembered, wasn't one of the countries that hated lords and elves.

She had choices, so she sat and followed the different paths of possibilities in her head as she watched the children play.

One was to sneak around the village and keep going the way she was going – but to where? She didn't know what lay down the road, and she had no end goal in mind. She wanted the EN to find her, and constantly moving wasn't going to help them do that. Her random roaming would mean they'd keep missing each other. The larger the village or town, the more likely she'd meet orcs or kidnappers, and the more a mob could overwhelm her.

This was a poor, backwater village at the edge of a jungle, and she could escape back to the jungle if she got into trouble. Lindy didn't survive through centuries of wars and witch hunts without always planning an escape route. That was second nature.

Or she could find a sympathetic person to help her, like the managers of the campgrounds or David. That had its own risks.

She could read futures, but unlike Judy, she couldn't read minds, and she could be lied to, or a helpful person could talk to someone with different ideas.

Or she could just walk the shit down the middle of the road like she was born there and play the Fairy Queen thing to the hilt. Hide in plain sight and hope to win over the villagers with a bit of magic theatre. If she did that, it would be all over the internet in fifteen minutes, and the EN would beeline here. If she got the mob on her side, any orcs or bad guys would have to think twice. If they thought she was a Glinda the Good Witch and not a demon from hell, it would work.

Lindy decided to trust the little girl's delighted reaction to her ears and go Full Fairy. She stood up, combed her fingers through her matted hair, and took a deep breath. She made sure she had a clean escape route to the forest and then stepped to the centre of the road and walked towards the village.

No one noticed her.

The kids played, the dogs slept, the old people squatted in the shade, gossiping and cleaning things in big, brightly-coloured plastic basins.

She walked by a grandma chopping at a huge jackfruit and stopped to watch. The old woman looked up and smiled at Lindy and then back down at the pods she was freeing from the pith so she wouldn't cut herself. Then suddenly she looked up again, freezing in mid-slice, and her jaw dropped.

"That looks good," said Lindy in Elvish. "But I'm getting tired of fruit. Do you know where I can get a sandwich? Something with meat?"

The woman slowly pointed down the street. Lindy thanked her and walked away.

There was a little sound behind her, and she turned to look. The children she'd seen playing were sneaking behind her, stalking her. When she turned, they all dove into doorways and behind parked cars. She walked a few more steps and could hear them giggling. And then she spun around, and they scattered, squealing.

Adults holding phones popped out of doorways and leaned out of windows. When she walked by or looked their way, they jumped back inside. No one said anything.

Another thirty feet or so, and she whirled around, and now there were twenty kids, and they screamed and ran off, laughing. One little girl stood in the middle of the road, confused by the game, and started to cry. Everyone had left her.

Lindy went back for her and squatted down and smiled. "Am I scary?" The girl shook her head. No.

"Good, because I want to see if I can find something to eat, like a sandwich, and I don't want to scare anyone."

Then she stood up and walked further into the village. There, in front of a small shop, was a street vendor selling *num pang* pate sandwiches. Just the thing.

She walked up to the skinny man standing next to his street food cart and laid it all out. She was very hungry and had no money, but she had friends coming soon, and they would pay for anything she ate. Would he trust her with a sandwich or two? For a minute, she didn't think he understood her; he just stood there and stared. Then he slowly nodded.

“Yes, Lady mrenh Kongveal, you eat all you want. On the house.” And he took a slow step back and then spun around and ran into the shop, slamming the door behind him.

So for the next two hours, Lindy sat by the cart and ate delicious pork pate sandwiches until she could barely move. By the time she stuffed down the last bite, Jameson knew exactly where she was, and RumLot Security had five undercover operatives screaming from the Mekong River to the village, over a hundred and twenty hard miles away.

It was, one said later, the most inconvenient route to the most inconvenient village in the most inconvenient of countries.

Soloyev

Estonia, a fitting place to regain Russia’s deserved glory.

Estonia, inhabited by humans for eleven thousand years, was the last place in Europe to give up the old ways.

Estonia, always struggling for independence, always trampled by larger countries that used its land as a bridge to conquer others, always resisting the rightful control of Russia.

Estonia, a tiny country of limited resources that unaccountably prospered while Russia, with its vast lands and natural resources, unfairly suffered. A proud country with one per cent of Russia’s population who thumbed their noses at Russians every single day. Simply by existing, the gnats of Estonia disrespected the supremacy of Mother Russia. It was galling.

Soloyev was absolutely sure his orcs could take over the republic the minute they breached the wall. There were only a few elf clans there and no lords. NATO wouldn’t come to their aid; it didn't exist anymore, and the untried EATO would dither until it was too late. France would block any help to faraway Estonia until they agreed to a resolution calling Russia naughty, and Soloyev would be raising a glass of champagne in a Tallinn restaurant when that happy event occurred.

Putin's big mistake in '22 had been taking on a huge swath of Ukraine, thinking he could overwhelm the massive country. If he had started with Estonia before Finland joined NATO, he would have walked in unopposed and had a win under his belt.

Now, Soloyev had a much harder job, but he was more intelligent, and he had orcs.

Soloyev was too intelligent to make the same mistake the demon lord had and inspect his forces in person. He had drones for that and a very good intelligence system embedded in Estonia. He even had spies working on the Wall itself. They reported that there were only about fifteen hundred elves living on the Estonian side and that included women and children who were, of course, useless in war. The Estonian Army was well-trained and well-armed, but they were few in number, too.

If Soloyev still owned a navy, he would have ordered warships in the Baltic to give the Estonians something to worry about on their north flank, but the navy had never recovered from the Ukrainian beating that decimated it, so all of the Estonian army was deployed on the Wall. It didn't matter; the Estonians were tiny, and they weren't orcs.

Soloyev put a hundred thousand orcs on the Estonian border, which was much, much more than he needed to overwhelm about ten thousand Estonian soldiers, and seven hundred volunteer elves. He also put two more armies of a hundred thousand each across the Donbas and on the Polish border just to keep the EN from getting bored.

At one in the morning, a band of Russian infiltrators hidden on the Estonian side snuck up to an Estonian guardpost at the base of the Wall and killed the guards – two Estonian reservists. After they called in their success, they took the elevator on the Estonian side to the top of the Wall, where they were supposed to eliminate the rest of the guards. That would allow a special force of orcs to use their drones to set up abseil points and scale the Wall and prepare an opening for their invasion.

That was the theory. What they didn't know was that the minute the two guards' heartbeats hit panic levels, the AI sensors in the guardpost alerted everyone from one end of Estonia's wall to the other. No lights, no sirens – the guards and soldiers knew they were being assaulted, and they moved to defend the Wall and protect Estonia, as they had obsessively trained for.

Soloyev was in his headquarters, watching the bank of video screens of drone feed. Then it winked out. Across Russia, great swaths of the electrical grid went down. The internet disappeared.

After watching the elves take down the Texas grid, he was prepared, and his own generators kicked in. When the internet and satellite feeds flickered back on, all that was on the screen was a jolly clown giving them the finger.

He grimaced at the unseriousness of his opponent. Clowns. It was undignified. Didn't they take war seriously? Didn't they take the power of Russia seriously?

The Russians moved to their backup communications – a wire strung across two thousand miles to the border, a single wire just like the old telegraphs used in the Great Patriotic War. Morse code telegraph operators began their work.

The news was not good. On top of the Wall, flashes of light were observed, and the seven hundred elves were quickly supplemented by thousands of elves of both genders, of all ages, busily and efficiently chopping off the heads of orcs who scaled the steep sides of the six-story barrier and reached the top. Orc heads were bouncing down the wall like Halloween pumpkins, and the rain of falling bodies knocked off the soldiers climbing up from below.

Elves and Estonian military snipers sat on tall chairs like tennis judges, shooting down Russian drones with sawed-off shotguns and protecting the decapitators at the wall face. Suddenly, they disappeared.

They weren't needed any more.

The EN drones flew in. Thousands of them, none needing any lights to see what they were doing as they all had night vision capability. They worked in AI-managed packs, hunting the soldiers waiting at the base of the wall, attacking Russian drones and support soldiers in the rear, as well as anyone who looked military and spoke Russian. Matt black, at night, they were almost invisible to the Russian soldiers, and with lethal, robotic efficiency, they systematically cut through the ranks, damaging the Russian orcs and killing the Russian humans. While many of the orcs were wounded, Soloyev knew they'd recover, but in the meantime, his army was being annihilated.

Then he turned to his artillery. He ordered the orcs scaling the Wall to retreat and authorised the big guns, ordering them to fire at the Wall with some special artillery shells his scientists had developed just for this scenario. If they couldn't go over the Wall, they would go through it.

The orcs stood down, and the telegraph operators relayed that the elves were disappearing. Winking out, they said. Soloyev wasn't fooled; they could be back in seconds. He waited for the report on the artillery.

Nothing happened.

Then the artillery telegraph operator tapped in "BLYAT!! – disappear! They wen –"

And that was the end of it. Soloyev didn't get any more news for four hours.

The artillery crews, guns, support, and even the food trucks had simply disappeared.

The hundred thousand orcs still at the base of the wall had been reduced to sixty thousand, and in the morning, they were still being hunted by EN drones. They didn't stop killing for three solid days, day and night.

The death toll stood at Estonia, 2 v Russia, 89,547.

Soloyev decided to rethink his tactics.

Adem and Malachi

When Adem pounded on his flat door, saying they had to go to fuckin' Estonia, Malachi was mad. When the little guy insisted on going behind fuckin' Russian lines, he was beside himself. When he told Malachi he either came and watched his back while he worked or he'd go by himself, unprotected, Malachi had a complete and total meltdown.

Adem just folded his arms and glared. You're the Warrior Lord, you love me, so protect me! He didn't actually say that; he just glared.

Finally, when Malachi was over his fit, he gave up and pulled his boots on, grumbling under his breath the entire time.

"Where the shit are we going?" And with that, a Warrior Elf ported them directly to a secret node Adem had set up ages ago with Sarah.

That's where it had all started, with Sarah. She was in James' office when the first reports of the Russian attack came in, and she saw it on the monitor on his office wall. Adem was supposed to meet her for a port to Ottawa – gods knew for what – something to do with Ayu – at one in the morning when he walked in looking for her, saw what was going on, and they both ran to the central control room.

The lords watched everything happening in real-time horror, and when the orcs backed down, the intel people knew exactly what would happen next. They even had an idea where the artillery was sitting, but they were waiting for it to light up their radars before they sent in their own missiles to take them out. Their plan was to intercept the Russian barrage with their ground-to-air defenses. Yeah, a few might get through, but not many, and they hoped the Russians didn't shoot and scoot so fast they couldn't be killed.

Adem knew how to make sure none got through. So he ported to Malachi, roused him out of bed, endured his meltdown, and there they were, twenty minutes later in fuckin' Russia, walking from a hidden transport node to the top of a hill. Then they threw themselves down on their stomachs and looked down at a brightly lit scene from Hell. Or a defense contractor's sales brochure. Same thing.

"So, what's the plan?" Malachi looked at Adem. "I don't think I can take them all."

Adem raised his head to get a better look, and Malachi slammed his head back down. "Keep your head down! Do you want to get us both killed? Your eyes are glowing!"

Adem looked at Malachi. "You might have to carry me back." Before Malachi could say that was a fantastic idea, let's go now, Adem flamed up. Just like that. And just like that, the entire artillery battery disappeared.

He grinned at Malachi. "WooHoo!!! It worked!"

Malachi looked at him in disbelief. Then he looked at the blank space, a perfect circle in the dirt about six inches deep where the battery used to be.

"You didn't know that would work?"

"No, but can we talk about this later? I really want to go home now." He stood up, wobbled, and then fell to his knees.

So Malachi picked him up, threw him over his shoulder, and carried him back to the transport node, where a warrior elf instantaneously popped in and ported them both back to Aelfeham House. A couple of housekeeper elves put Adem to bed, and Malachi went back to his own room and resumed sleeping. It took a while.

Ayu and Jameson

It was a helicopter. It looked like a dragonfly, only not as sturdy. General Jameson was patient and stood on the helipad at

Phnom Penh International Airport and watched the lord glare at the copter with undisguised distaste.

Lord Ayu knew the facts. The village where Lindy sat emerged from the jungle was at least five hours away by car on some pretty dire, indirect roads. They were about an hour away by helicopter. The EN had hired every private helicopter in the area, and the soldiers (renamed bodyguards for the sensibilities of the Cambodian government) were already loading up. There were undercover operatives already on the way to secure Lord Aethelind's safety, but they were going by road, and it would take them hours, too.

Walking would take longer, even for a lord with magical powers. Usually, Ayu walked everywhere, but then he usually had all the time in the world (literally). If he knew that Lindy was safe, he'd either walk or ride a horse or some other pack animal. An elephant, maybe.

Or he could have a big wind blow him there, but that would cause other problems, and in any case, the altitude and the air pressure still made him violently airsick. And a strong wind would mess up the other helicopters, endangering the humans who were trying to help him.

He groaned in frustration and then suddenly sprinted to the helicopter before he thought about it too much. Jameson had to run behind him, yelling to duck! Damn! The last thing the general needed was a lord decapitated by a helicopter blade. That wouldn't look good in the after-action reports.

Soth Dany

The kids sat and played around Lindy as she ate the sandwiches, coming up to her to stare, ask a question, and then run off to think about it for a while. After about half an hour of this, she was no longer weird-fairy-lady but just Lord Aethelind, a name they thought was very funny and very hard to pronounce. They made up songs and played hopscotch to the odd syllables.

The adults took a bit longer, but eventually they wandered out. They weren't afraid that Lindy would hurt them; that's why they let the kids stay out and play around her. She was good luck! But she was magic, and magic was by definition unknown and uncontrollable. The teenagers came out first and hung around, watching the lord eat and taking hundreds of videos and pictures to upload onto their social media accounts.

After thinking about it, the old grandmas and grandpas of the village knew Lindy really wasn't a mrenh kongveal because only children could see the creatures, and obviously, older people could see this person, too. And she was too tall. But after a couple of hours of watching the lord, they weren't worried about her. She meant no harm, and her people were on their way to pick her up. They sat back, relaxed, and watched the show. They hadn't had this much excitement in the village since Pol Pot died in '98.

The photos were immediately seen by elf-fans worldwide, and overloaded servers in Cambodia started to crash with the heavy traffic, but not before a drug lord and smuggler based in a town forty miles away noticed what was going on.

Soth Dany had a nice, small-time operation moving drugs and other interesting goods between Laos and Cambodia as part of a chain of mid-level gangsters who operated up and down the quiet back roads that threaded between China and the ports of Vietnam. Many of the trucks advertising vegetables and other goods that Lindy observed on the road when she was watching were his. But they weren't hauling mangos.

But here, on his patch, had just occurred a fantastic stroke of good luck! A mrenh kongveal was lucky, but even luckier was a lord, a magical creature who was worth real money to the right people. A woman who didn't show any heavy-duty magic or she wouldn't be stuck in a fuckin' muddy hellhole on Hwy 76. Even his trucks didn't stop there for gas or lunch. It was a pass-through village holding nothing of interest to anyone. Until today!

He sent a squad of his best people to go pick her up. Put a bag over her head, he said, so she can't see them, and they'd be okay. And don't hurt her. He wanted her with no bruises or scars, to keep her value. No raping. He didn't want her used up.

They were only an hour away, and in the meantime, he made some discreet inquiries. No one he knew would actually want to keep her, but every level up the retail chain would take a cut and sell her on to a middleman closer to the end buyer. Who knew where she would end up, but that wasn't Soth's concern. Like the drugs and the illegal arms he moved, what the end user did with the goods was their own business.

Lindy

The old lady who Lindy first met when she was cleaning the jackfruit brought the lord an IZE cola, and after that, the adults started hanging around, asking questions, and making polite conversation. Lindy told them that she expected her clan, the EN, to come pick her up very soon because she saw all the kids putting her picture on social media. The EN would see the posts right away, but she didn't know how long it would take. Maybe a couple of days. England was a long way away.

That seemed reasonable to everyone, and they started talking among themselves about where she could stay in the meantime, who had an extra bed, that sort of thing. While the kids played and the teenagers tapped on their phones, the adults talked about practical matters like how they were going to take care of this exotic guest.

With most of the villagers gathered in front of the tiny shop, there was soon a holiday atmosphere. Someone asked Lindy if she could really do magic, and with her decision to go full Fairy Queen and get them on her side (which seemed to be working, so far), she agreed to one ("only once, because magic is very tiring") demonstration. She levitated a couple of the kids a few feet and flew them around in a circle, leaving them laughing so hard they couldn't breathe. After that, no matter how hard they teased and begged, she wouldn't do it again because Lindy was an old performer, and she knew that you always left them wanting a bit more. Once was enough.

The party in the middle of town, the magic demonstration, the lord who sat and talked to them – it was all very distracting, and when Soth's men drove into town, no one saw them until they were at the edge of the crowd, sitting and standing around their truck watching the lord. They were the only people not smiling.

Two of them were orcs.

Two of Soth's guys went into the shop where they were immediately recognised, but it was too late. Without a word, they pointed guns at the people in there and herded them to the back, out of the way. The older ones had lived through Pol Pot and the Khmer Rouge, and long, sad experience had taught them that when a man with dead eyes points a gun at you and tells you to leave, you leave.

At some signal, the rest of the gang rushed Lindy, and an almost silent ripple of terror passed through the crowd as the villagers grabbed their kids and parted like a shoal of minnows fleeing from a shark.

Startled, Lindy hesitated as she identified the thugs running at her through the children, and then everything went black. One of the shop guys came from behind, and then a burlap fruit bag was over her head, so she couldn't see where to aim her magic. With the villagers and their kids mixed in with her attackers, a general blast was out of the question.

But it wasn't the first time she'd been jumped like this.

She went limp and let them take her away.

Grinning and hooting, the victorious gangsters were sure she'd fainted. The stupid fairy-woman didn't even struggle! They threw her in the back of the truck, zip-tied her wrists and ankles, and with a few warning gunshots in the air to remind the villagers who was boss, they turned and sped off with their prize. It was an easy operation, just as the boss had said it would be, and now they had a good-luck fairy under wraps. What they really had in the bag was a furious, wide-awake lord waiting for the first free minute away from the village to escape, and when she escaped, she wouldn't take any prisoners. She didn't need the extra baggage.

The bag was burlap, and once her eyes adjusted, Lindy could make out shapes through the loose weave. She lay in the back of a short-bed truck, bouncing around as it sped over the rough road, with two men sitting next to her. There was a stinking *beng* just feet away from her, and she could see his outline against the bright sky as he stood guard at the cab of the truck, holding a stubby machine gun of some sort. With the wind of the truck flowing back, she had the joy of experiencing his reek, but he had fresh air and couldn't smell her.

About ten minutes out of town, the truck slowed down to avoid a huge pothole, and someone grabbed her leg, and she heard a gunshot. The hand released her leg, and the two men sitting next to her, cursing and screaming, yelled for the driver to stop.

The beng had smelled her lord's scent when the truck slowed down and gave in to his genetic orc instinct to kill, rape or eat a lord and grabbed her, but one of the other kidnappers immediately shot him. They were upset; now they'd have to explain the beng's death to their boss. But the boss ordered that no scars, no bruises, no fooling around with the goods, and if Seo went crazy and decided to disobey the boss, that was his problem.

With the villagers well out of range now and with her guards down to two distracted and upset thugs, Lindy decided this escapade had gone on long enough. The zip-ties around her wrists and ankles quietly snapped in half all by themselves. A small hole developed in the burlap bag, and if a kidnapper had looked through closely, he would have seen a glowing, green eye peering out.

The man she could see suddenly gasped, looked confused, and then slumped. The other guy didn't notice. Now she was down to one sitting with her and the two men in the cab. She turned, the bag ripped off her head, the guard looked at the lord, and in his last terror-filled seconds of life saw her furious witch's eyes and knew he was dead. And he was, his head bouncing down the road behind the truck like a grisly soccer ball.

Lindy sat up, knelt at the window of the cab, and politely knocked. The driver looked into his rear view mirror, and the lord looked back, smiling but not smiling, her body glowing and her eyes green lasers.

She told him to stop the truck; Lindy didn't fancy ploughing into a tree when she jerked off this guy's head. The truck skidded to a stop, and his partner turned, screamed, burst out of the door and tripped, and before he hit the ground, his own head was rolling down the road. Now, all of the orcs had been taken out. That left the driver escaping into the forest, but Lindy wasn't feeling generous that day, not like she was with that night watchman so many years ago. She ripped the driver in two with a blast of furious lord power that came so fast he didn't know he was dead until he saw the Gates of the Void opening before him.

The road was still with the silence that comes with death, and all the lord could hear was the sound of trees, wind, and her own rasping breath. Lindy hopped off the truck and thought about her options. Walk back to the village? There might be other witch hunters there, but that's where the EN would come to find her, and she was sure in her heart that she had made enough noise for her friends to notice and rescue her. She had to stay in the area and watch for them. But she would have to stay hidden and not put the villagers in danger if people were trying to kill her, because that was the last thing she wanted to do. They were kind to her.

She didn't want Ayu to come looking for her; he was busy fixing the world, and besides, she wanted him safe at Aelfeham House. Or physically safe at least; Lindy wasn't so sure about romantically safe. She thought about him all the time and had a niggling suspicion that she was on the way to bonding with him, and that wasn't good, not if it was a one-way bond. The only way to find out was to spend more time with him. He was a shaper of worlds who had never bonded, and she was a witch who attracted murderers and rapists whenever she turned around, so her odds weren't good. Men who weren't trying to kill her didn't like her, and shapers of worlds had better things to do than deal with high-maintenance survivors.

But Gaia had said she would find someone one day and not to be too down on herself. Lindy smiled wryly. But then Gaia had given her the magic stick, and *that* had turned out to be a dud, so maybe listening to the Gatekeeper to the Void muse on love might not be a fruitful way to spend her time.

She would walk into the jungle and watch the village in secret. Like with her Romani clans, she would guard the villagers from witch hunters and attackers when she could, but she couldn't stay with them, not while she was being hunted herself.

Ah well, she thought. It was good while it lasted. The village was now ten miles away and a good hike through the jungle; best get started while there was still light.

Jameson and Ayu

It was like something out of a war movie; helicopters landed all around the village, disgorging men in full body armour and really nasty weapons – and nothing to do. The older villagers who had lived through war and Pol Pot were not amused, but the young ones thought it was cool.

There was a lord with them. A tall man (especially when compared to the average Cambodian, even the young ones who had good food growing up) with huge ears, bright blue glowing eyes, and a foul expression on his face.

When the RumLot agents talked to the villagers, Jameson was reminded of elves when they were asked about something they really didn't want to talk about. They didn't say no or lie; they just talked around the subject and concentrated on just about anything else. The villagers didn't want to tell the stern, glowing-eyed lord what had happened to his woman. What if he got mad at them? Nor did they want to piss off Soth Dany by fingering him as the kidnapper (they all knew who the thugs were). They had to live with him later, and he had a long memory.

So they danced around, suddenly remembered they had laundry soaking that needed to be hung out to dry, missed dental appointments, bad memories, they were taking a shit when everything happened – all that sort of thing.

It took a good half hour to find out what had actually happened and which direction the kidnappers had gone, and then the soldiers had to decide who was going to stay in the village and who was going to get back in the helicopter and go to Soth's compound. By the time Jameson was finished with that and looked for Lord Ayu, the lord was gone.

Now he had two missing lords, and all he could do was throw up his hands and tell the helicopter pilots to watch for the lord as they flew over the road. When they found him, they would stop and pick him up.

Ayu

Trotting down the road, Ayu sniffed, and ever so faintly, he could smell Lindy. While Jameson was running around organising his men, Ayu waited at the front of the little shop where she'd sat and eaten, and the ache he felt from missing her was physically painful. He could smell her scent, hear her heart, and he knew she was alive and close by.

Although the adults were afraid of him, the children weren't, and they told him straight out what had happened and where she was being taken, and that was enough. He wasn't going to wait for Jameson, and he certainly wasn't going to go back in a helicopter again.

Well, he admitted to himself, he would if it meant life or death for Lindy, but not for anything else. Those things were nightmares.

By the time Jameson noticed the lord was missing, Ayu was already three miles down the road, and he could smell the orc scent lingering in the air and the equally foul scent of the truck. The Lindy scent was normal, though. No fear in the scent, just her.

The tracks of the truck got sharper as the ground got muddier. He skirted a big puddle, and then around a bend and sitting up in the middle of the road was a befuddled orc. He was damaged, but not dead and was quickly recovering from some injury that had left a big stain of blood on his chest, shoulder, and arm. Good gods, he was foul, and Ayu didn't slow down as he trotted by. He left the man-monster sitting in the middle of the road, staring at the back of the lord. Once Ayu was out of splatter range, the orc exploded, his head nicely separating from his body. Ayu didn't look back.

Another mile and he passed a human's head, and that cheered him up considerably. Lindy was fighting back! He could still smell her, and the scent was getting stronger. She still wasn't fearful – but now he could smell her anger, and that was good, too. Much better to be angry than afraid.

Then he saw it, the truck. He walked up, spotting a fly-covered body on his left, the torso with the exposed spine almost ten feet away from the bottom half with the legs. Boy, she must have been pissed! To his right, the flies were feasting on a headless orc. In the bed of the truck was a dead man with no visible injuries, and a leftover headless body. The phone in the corpse's pocket was buzzing, but wouldn't be taking any more incoming calls as the owner was permanently unavailable.

All dead. No Lindy, but also no scent of an injured or scared Lindy. Just a pissed one who had escaped into the brush. Almost dancing with joy, Ayu circled like a scent hound, sniffing and listening for her. She couldn't be far. He could hear her heartbeat when he stopped and concentrated.

Ayu stopped and texted Jameson. "Escaped; don't risk men." And he ran off into the jungle.

He didn't hear her; he didn't see her; he only felt her when she leapt on him and screamed with joy.

"AYU!!!" And there she was, in his arms, her legs wrapped tight around his waist, and almost knocking him over with her kisses. Not that he minded at all.

"You came for me!" She kissed him again and sobbed, burying her face in his neck, and he laughed and danced and clutched her tight to him, not letting her get down.

"Of course I did! You haunt my dreams! You were calling me! How could I leave you here alone?"

Lindy hugged him hard, and this time she kissed him on the mouth, slowly, and that changed the mood entirely from ecstatic joy to something much more intimate.

"You came for me, and now I'm not alone," she whispered, and her eyes were bright with tears.

Ayu's voice shook. "I'll always come for you, Aethelind, and you'll never be alone if that's what you want. If you'll have me."

That's all it took. The Fortuneteller couldn't read her own fortune, but at that moment she knew her own future. She cried, and with the first gulp of air as she sobbed, she bonded. When Ayu felt her heat, he kissed her and completed his bond, too.

On their way back to the village, they heard a huge boom. Sarah had homed in on Jameson and ported in with Adem, and he made a transport node. Within minutes, transport elves appeared in the node area, and the villagers had the joy of seeing real, correctly-sized mrenh kongveal, and Ayu had the great relief of porting back to Aelfeham House instead of returning on the jet.

A month later, Soth Dany received an invitation to visit the village as an honoured guest at the Khmer New Year festival. Thinking it would be a good thing to go and re-establish his gangster creds with the locals so they didn't get any upstart ideas, he put on his best suit and, with a platoon of formidable bodyguards, strutted through the crowded festival and down the centre of town as if he owned the place, which he did. The minute he walked over the invisible area that Adem had turned into a transport node, there was a flash of sparkles, the briefest glimpse of a really bad-ass Warrior Elf, and Soth disappeared.

He simply flashed away.

A minute later, his head reappeared, rolling down the street like a bowling ball. Just the head.

A minute after that, his body reappeared.

And that was the end of Soth Dany.

Soloyev and Meechum

The Estonian debacle didn't discourage the Russians; they said it was just a test anyway. A live fire exercise to see if their experimental weapons worked. They weren't even trying hard.

They never figured out what happened to the artillery battalion, and by the time a week had passed, it had officially never existed. Soloyev had all mention of it wiped clean from all public and military records as "EN disinformation". It puzzled the Russian intel people that there was no evidence of any lord activity like burning, boiling, or slicing. Their guys just disappeared. Soon, everyone in the senior ranks convinced themselves that the men on the field that night simply defected with their equipment and that the EN had bought them off. The alternative, that the EN could just "disappear" seven hundred soldiers and their equipment, was just too awful and bizarre to contemplate.

Unfortunately for the Russians, the European Alliance was strengthened by the Russian attack. Now, renewed Russian aggression wasn't just a theory; it was a fact, and that concentrated minds in Brussels. As James said to Sarah, it was like every couple of decades, the diplomats in Brussels had to have a wake-up call because as soon as peace broke out, they all developed war amnesia.

Meechum and his supporters in the US, on the other hand, were horrified at the strength shown by the EN. It was unethical, they said, to use magic in a war to kill people. They saw no difference in the EN using magic to defend itself and its allies against the semi-magical orcs than if they'd used biological warfare. They promptly passed laws in the US to make the use of magic as an offensive weapon illegal and pressed the UN to support a resolution condemning it, and requested that the UN set up a system of inspectors to verify that no magic was being developed and weaponised.

No one paid any attention to them.

But Meechum saw real benefit to the US if the EN was occupied with a hot war in Europe against the Russians, and he personally thought it was a good way to keep Russia neutralised, too. So he supported easing of all sanctions "for humanitarian reasons" and as a way to "combat the spread of demons" and so permitted US businesses to export technology, arms, and fast food to Russia. Soloyev was very, very pleased with that, and to his mind, losing eighty-five thousand orcs was well worth the sacrifice if it got the US to lift sanctions.

Lindy and Ayu

Two days after they arrived at Aelfeham House, Ayu was having lunch in their flat and looking over topographical maps of Cambodia, trying to figure out the best way to increase the range of the golden-cheeked monkeys, when Lindy sat down beside him.

"Here. I'm supposed to give this to my bond-man when I find him, and I guess you're nominated." Lindy gave him a wry smile. "It's not much to look at, I'm afraid." And she set Gaia's Magic Chopstick down on his map.

Frowning, he picked it up. "Where did you get this?"

"Gaia gave it to me when I was dead."

He looked at her, his eyes inscrutable. "You saw Gaia when you were dead?"

Lindy sighed. "Yeah, I don't like to talk about being dead, but I was dead. Didn't you wonder where I was before I showed up in Cambodia? Did you think I ported there?"

"I don't like talking about you being dead, either. We weren't completely bonded then, and I thought I was misinterpreting." Then he looked at the stick. "I don't know what I thought, really. The last thing I wanted to think about was you being dead. But I knew you were dead, then you weren't dead, and I could feel you."

"I was dead as dead can be and sitting outside the Gates of the Void, watching Gaia. She's the Gatekeeper. Something about atoning for her sins. She sits at the Gates and lets people in, I guess. She morphs every few seconds, but she always holds this stick." Lindy tilted her head as she looked at her bond-man, wondering what he was thinking. "Anyway, it wasn't my time yet. But to pass the time I had there, we talked about a lot of things. She wanted to trade fortunes – I would tell hers, and she would tell mine.

"She liked hers; she was very happy with it. But when she read mine, she was upset and disappeared for a while. When she came back, she said to keep her stick."

Lindy tapped the stick on the map. "I started calling it Gaia's Magic Chopstick. She said, *"The stick is magic; it will help you get through any troubles on the way to your forever man. When you meet him, give him the stick, and he'll know what to do with it.*" Pfft – it didn't do a bit of magic. It didn't help get me through any troubles, not at all. No food, no directions. Not even a warning about the beng! It was completely useless and just got in the way. But I'm following through with my promise. You're my forever man, and here's the stick. What are you going to do with it?"

Ayu looked at the stick; he knew what it was the minute he picked it up. It was Gaia's bond-pin. When she bonded and he didn't, he didn't give her a pin, so she just went out and got her own, a very Gaia thing to do. She didn't want to look unbonded, and she wanted everyone to think her bond was just like every other woman's. She never gave him a bond-knife, either, because in the end it was all about appearances – hers. The bond-pin was a lie just like their bonding had been a lie.

The pin went to the Gates with her, and now it was back. She didn't have a proper funeral pyre to throw it on, so it had stayed with her, a permanent reminder of her arrogance.

He certainly wasn't going to give it as a bond-pin to Lindy; she deserved her own, one that didn't look like a chopstick a puppy had played with.

Gaia must have known when she read Lindy's fortune that he and Lindy would bond.

"*Give this to your forever man.*"

He held it between two fingers and looked at it, a worn, rather ugly chopstick. Gaia had said it was magic, but there was no magic in this piece of wood. It was useless, but then it always had been. Maybe saying it was magic was another lie to keep Lindy from throwing it away when it was a pain in the ass to keep. She'd badly wanted Lindy to give this to him.

Why? To free him? He was already free; he had never bonded. Or to tell him she no longer claimed Ayu, that *she* was free of him. It didn't matter in the end; past was past, and she was working through her past sins, and he was probably one of them.

Lindy watched Ayu frown at the stick and started to worry. Was this some trick of Gaia's? Was she interfering in her new life?

Ayu looked up, smiled at his bond-wife, and then broke the pin in two and tossed it in the fireplace. Gaia was right; he did know what to do with it.

End of Book 9

Book 10

Captain of Our Fairy Band

Continue the adventure!

This and all books in

The Return of the Tribes Series

are available for download on

Amazon Kindle
or
The Rum Lot Publishing

www.rumlot.com

E-Publishing, Hardback and Paperback versions of all books are available on amazon.com

Please Donate to the Excelsior Trust

If you enjoyed this book (and we hope you did!), please consider a small donation to The Excelsior Trust, a registered charity that is dedicated to preserving heritage fishing boats, in particular The Excelsior, LT 472, a wonderful fishing smack that is featured in Book Two.

As part of the trust's mission to preserve Britain's maritime heritage, they also subsidise unique training and sailing experiences for young people.

https://www.theexcelsiortrust.co.uk/

https://www.theexcelsiortrust.co.uk/donate
Registered Charity Number 285899

www.ingramcontent.com/pod-product-compliance
Lightning Source LLC
Chambersburg PA
CBHW070744180626

46818CB00007B/2988
9781918079258